Hovering over her, one hand splayed on the bed by her waist, his chiseled jaw tight, his chest rose before Amadeo lowered his face and kissed her.

In all Elsbeth's fantasies about their first kiss, she'd imagined how it would feel. She'd imagined it would be warm and that it would feel nice. The last thing she'd expected was the crackle of electricity that shot through her.

This was more than *nice*...

Closing her eyes, she thrilled as the pressure of his mouth deepened and his hands began to roam over her body. Yes, this felt far, far more than nice, especially when he cupped her breast, and she squeezed her eyes tighter and reminded herself of her mother's words that she was only to be compliant.

For all her mother's words, though, it was hard to stop herself from shivering with pleasure when he gathered the hem of her nightdress and tugged it up to her hips, his hand skimming the flesh of her inner thigh. Every brush of his skin against hers felt like fire. Delicious fire.

Scandalous Royal Weddings

Marriages to make front-page news!

Raised on the Mediterranean island kingdom of Ceres, Princes Amadeo and Marcelo and Princess Alessia want for nothing. But with their life of luxury comes an impeccable reputation to uphold. Any hint of a scandal could turn the eyes of the world on them...and force them down the royal aisle! Their lives may be lived in the spotlight, but only one person will have the power to truly see them...

When Prince Marcelo rescues Clara from a forced wedding, he simultaneously risks a diplomatic crisis and his heart.

Read on in
Crowning His Kidnapped Princess

Billionaire Gabriel may fix scandals for a living, but his night with Princess Alessia creates a scandal of their own when she discovers she's pregnant!

Read on in
Pregnant Innocent Behind the Veil

Prince Amadeo must face a stranger at the altar when convenient royal wedding bells chime.

Read on in
Rules of Their Royal Wedding Night

Don't miss this scandalous trilogy
by Michelle Smart!

All available now!

Michelle Smart

—

RULES OF THEIR ROYAL WEDDING NIGHT

HARLEQUIN
PRESENTS

HARLEQUIN®
PRESENTS™

PLEASE RECYCLE · PRODUCT IS RECYCLABLE

Recycling programs
for this product may
not exist in your area.

ISBN-13: 978-1-335-58404-5

Rules of Their Royal Wedding Night

Copyright © 2022 by Michelle Smart

Harlequin Enterprises ULC
22 Adelaide St. West, 41st Floor
Toronto, Ontario M5H 4E3, Canada
www.Harlequin.com

Printed in U.S.A.

Michelle Smart's love affair with books started when she was a baby and would cuddle them in her cot. A voracious reader of all genres, she found her love of romance established when she stumbled across her first Harlequin book at the age of twelve. She's been reading them—and writing them—ever since. Michelle lives in Northamptonshire, England, with her husband and two young Smarties.

Books by Michelle Smart

Harlequin Presents

Stranded with Her Greek Husband
Claiming His Baby at the Altar

Billion-Dollar Mediterranean Brides

The Forbidden Innocent's Bodyguard
The Secret Behind the Greek's Return

Christmas with a Billionaire

Unwrapped by Her Italian Boss

Scandalous Royal Weddings

Crowning His Kidnapped Princess
Pregnant Innocent Behind the Veil

Visit the Author Profile page
at Harlequin.com for more titles.

CHAPTER ONE

ELSBETH FERNANDEZ STEPPED into Ceres Cathedral, her arm held by her cousin, Dominic. Why he gripped it so tightly was beyond her. She'd been nothing but compliant with his wishes that she marry Prince Amadeo. She was always compliant. King of her home principality, Monte Cleure, Dominic's word was law, especially for the female members of his family.

Her handsome prince, who she'd met only once at their pre-wedding party, stood far in the distance. Their marriage had been agreed, like everything else in her life, without Elsbeth's input, but when the man tasked with negotiating the marriage had privately asked if she was willing, she hadn't hesitated to say yes. In all honesty, her prince could be the ugliest man in the world and she would still have agreed to marry him, so it was her good fortune that he was the handsomest prince in Europe.

He was so tall! She'd marvelled at the height difference between them and secretly delighted that he stood a foot taller than Dominic. He didn't look to have an ounce of fat on him either, unlike her obese cousin and the majority of the male members of the House of Fernandez, who liked to gorge. Her prince—and Elsbeth had taken to privately, gleefully, referring to him as *her* prince since the order had come for her to marry him— had a body that was indisputably hard. Sculpted. His face had a sculpted quality to it too with its chiselled jawline, accentuated bow of the top lip and long, straight nose.

She hoped he would be a kind husband. Or at least as kind as a royal prince used to his word being law could be. Elsbeth knew her duty as a future king's wife was to follow her husband's lead in all matters, speak only when spoken to, never give an opinion on anything weightier than flower arrangements, never disagree with her husband in public or in private and, most importantly, breed as many children as her husband desired. She prayed she was fertile. She would hate to disappoint him on any matter but a failure to breed would be classed as unforgivable and could see her divorced and sent back to Monte Cleure. It had happened to her aunt. Three years of a childless marriage and she'd been set aside and replaced with a new model.

Please let me give my prince children. Don't give him an excuse to send me back to Monte Cleure.

Since their pre-wedding party, she'd prayed nightly that God grant her prince children, and then she'd closed her eyes and drifted into sleep, happily conjuring his clear green eyes and the black lashes surrounding them, and imagining what those firm but full lips would feel like pressed against her own and what his thick black hair would feel like threaded through her fingers.

The urge to run down the aisle to her prince was strong but Elsbeth maintained her steady pace by reminding herself that when she left this cathedral she would no longer be under Dominic's subjugation.

While she knew much about the public image of the Berruti royal family and the workings of its reigning queen to ensure their relevance in the twenty-first century, she knew little about its private workings or the kind of man her prince was behind closed doors. Whatever the future held for her, it couldn't be worse than her lot in the House of Fernandez. God wouldn't be so cruel. Would He…?

Amadeo watched his bride make her way sedately down the aisle towards him, her arm linked with the man he despised most in the world, and made sure to keep his revulsion at both of them far from his face. The only positive he could take from this union was that Elsbeth was pretty. Very pretty, he grudgingly admitted. Her silky blonde hair had been elegantly swept off her oval face and as she walked closer to him the excitement was evident in her big blue eyes and the smile of her wide, plump mouth.

She'd displayed the same excitement at their pre-wedding party, the one and only time he'd met her. And yet, for all her smiles, which had quickly become grating, she'd hardly said a word. Not once had she started a conversation. She'd answered direct questions with a smile that didn't falter but seemed not to have a single opinion or idea in her head.

Already sickened at being stuck with a Fernandez for the rest of his life and becoming a relation by law to the tyrannical, narcissistic, megalomaniac Dominic, his bride being a wilting wallflower only added to his antipathy at the situation. There had been no alternative though, not with their two nations on the brink of a full-blown trade and diplomatic war. Amadeo's brother had lit the fire. Then, just as it was brought under control, his sister had thrown a can of petrol on it. This marriage was the only way to extinguish the fire in its entirety. For the sake of his nation, the monarchy he would one day head and his family, Amadeo was prepared to marry his enemy's cousin. His whole life had been spent doing what was best for the monarchy, his human inclinations and desires stifled into submission.

If his siblings had stifled their desires and inclinations more effectively, he wouldn't be standing here now.

His bride reached him.

As heir to the throne, Amadeo had always known the priority when he came to choose a bride would be suitability. After all, his wife would one day be Queen Consort and a figurehead for his great nation. Elsbeth's breeding made her highly suitable for the role. He had though, expected to marry someone he could like and respect and whose company he enjoyed. Of those three traits, Elsbeth ticked the box of none.

Conscious that this most magnificent of occasions was being broadcast into the home of every Ceresian not lining the streets and into the homes of many Italians and other Europeans, he reached for her small hand and bestowed her with a practised smile. Baby blue eyes sparkling as brightly as the diamonds on her tiara, she returned his smile with an eagerness that made his stomach turn. With over a hundred million eyes watching his reaction though, he hid it, playing up for the cameras by mouthing, truthfully, 'You look beautiful.'

She blushed at the compliment in a manner the cameras would adore. No doubt the cameras already adored her. He could already imagine the comments from the gushing reporters about the fairy-tale wedding dress the bride was wearing, all white lace and silk, emphasising but not displaying her generous bust—not a hint of cleavage was on display—and enhancing her slender waist before the skirt splayed out in the shape of a flamenco fan.

Hands clasped together, they turned their backs on the packed congregation and faced the bishop.

Elsbeth had never known cheers and applause like it. The streets lined with well-wishers had been loud on her entrance to the cathedral but when they came back out the sound would have taken any roof off.

A row of horse-drawn carriages awaited them. Her romantic husband assisted her into the first one and then, once seated beside her, took her hand in his.

The journey back to the castle seemed to go on for ever, and so did the applause. These people were genuinely happy for them, she realised with amazement as she blew a kiss to a frantically waving child being carried on her father's shoulders. Her husband's people cheered them all the way to the castle gates, and by the time they reached it her cheeks hurt from smiling and her wrist ached from all the waving.

Feeling as if she were in the most fantastical dream, she stood beside Amadeo to greet their guests, from the important to the not-so-important. There were so many heads of state and A-list celebrities that the castle's roofs were thronged with snipers and the surrounding grounds thick with heavily armed security. Inside the castle though, the banqueting room their twelve-course meal was being held in was a mass of glittering gold and silver, and any security was unobtrusive enough to melt into the background.

She tried so hard to take everything in so future Elsbeth could dip into her memory bank whenever she wanted, but her dreamlike state was such that the only thing she could focus on with anything like clarity was her new husband. He was just so charming! Having lived her life in a royal palace infested with charming snakes, she wasn't naive enough to think the charm was anything but a public act but he was being attentive to her, constantly checking that she liked the food and that she had enough to drink. Not only was he a prince but a gentleman!

Her mother's watchful gaze though, was a reminder that, gentleman or not, her husband, a future king, had expectations and standards he expected her to adhere to, and that Elsbeth must abide by them from the start. She wasn't foolish enough to do anything less.

Hours later, their meal over, it was time to move to a stateroom for the wedding reception party. Glad to have Amadeo holding her hand, she let him lead her to a table and tried not to overtly marvel at how exquisitely the room had been adorned. The colour scheme followed on from the banqueting room and yet managed to be even glitzier.

She caught the eye of her new brother-in-law's wife, Clara, who gave her such a beaming smile it made Elsbeth's belly warm with pleasure. Dominic had kidnapped Clara some months back and would have forced her to marry him if Amadeo's brother, Marcelo, hadn't rescued her and married her himself. Elsbeth had been terrified of meeting her at the pre-wedding party but her fears had been unfounded, Clara welcoming her generously and with no hint she blamed Elsbeth for Dominic's cruel, unconscionable actions.

Her new sister-in-law, Alessia, had been very welcoming at the pre-wedding party too, although Elsbeth thought she looked a little distracted today. It warmed her belly even more to think these nice women were her new family. Maybe one day they would be her friends too. She could hope. She hoped for lots of things.

Elsbeth's prince leaned into her and murmured, 'It is time for us to dance.'

A frisson raced up her spine and, her heart bolting into a canter, she rose to her feet. With her hand enveloped in Amadeo's, and catcalls and whistles from the increasingly raucous crowd, who'd been guzzling champagne as if it were going out of fashion, she walked to the centre of the dance floor.

One hand held in his, she put the other lightly

on his shoulder. Another, deeper frisson careered through her when his hand slipped around her waist to rest on her lower back.

Her heart thumping too hard and too fast for anything more than the underlying beat of the romantic song they danced to to register, Elsbeth could hardly draw breath. The first time she'd danced with Amadeo she'd been too excited at the thought of escaping Monte Cleure to think of anything other than not screwing it up by making a bad impression on him. This time she'd had a month since their first dance and had done little but dream of him. To be in his arms, her breasts pressed lightly into his hard stomach, her senses filling with his scent, was enough to send her into overdrive.

Amadeo danced with his new wife until the dance floor was so crowded their bodies were crushed together. She didn't utter a single word, simply kept the fixed smile on her face that had been ever-present since she'd arrived at the cathedral. Did she even have thoughts in that pretty head or was it only air?

'Shall we get a drink?' he suggested, dipping his head to speak into her ear over the growing noise. He caught a light, delicate scent that perfectly suited his insipid bride. It turned his stomach.

'If you like,' she replied brightly.

Mentally gritting his teeth, he led her—she didn't make the first move to leave the dance floor, just as she hadn't made the first move on anything at all that day, always waiting for him to take the lead—back to their table. She'd finished her glass of wine during the wedding breakfast by the end of the fourth course, but had made no effort to call any of the waiting staff over to refill it for her. He was certain the glass would have remained empty if he hadn't asked if she would like some more. She'd responded with a bright smile and a 'Yes, please.'

What had he married? A walking, talking, wind-up doll like his sister used to play with when she was a child?

When they reached their table and fresh drinks had been brought to them, his brother, Marcelo, caught his eye and nodded to the dance floor. Following his gaze, Amadeo saw the tall figure of their new brother-in-law, Gabriel. A gap in the crowd gave him a glimpse of their tiny sister wrapped tightly in Gabriel's arms.

A small breath of relief escaped his lungs. Gabriel had negotiated the wedding contract between Amadeo and Elsbeth. He'd also had a one-night stand with Alessia that had resulted in a baby-sized consequence. Amadeo and their parents had emotionally blackmailed Alessia into marrying him. It had ended in disaster a week ago when Alessia had kicked Gabriel out of the castle and told him to never come back. Normally, Amadeo would have taken it on himself to bring them back together for the good of the monarchy but his sister had been so distraught over the collapse of her short marriage that, for once, he'd held off from interfering. The way they held each other told him his instinct to hold back had been right as they'd obviously found their way back together without his assistance.

Taking a large gulp of his champagne, he watched Marcelo take a cheeky grab of Clara's bottom, and saw Clara's response, a mock slap of the hand followed by a passionate kiss on the lips. Theirs was a marriage Amadeo had emotionally blackmailed them into making too. As with Alessia and Gabriel, love had found them. And happiness. What Marcelo and Clara shared was a happiness he sometimes envied.

Sometimes too, his envy tasted bitter.

Marcelo had been allowed to escape the confines of royal life for a decade, joining the Ceres army and thriving amidst all the adventures that life had brought. It would have been out of the question for Amadeo to do the same. He was the heir. Every step he took and every word he spoke and every action he made was done with the dignity of his role at the forefront of his mind. It was beyond the realms of credulity that he would have swooped in to rescue a kidnapped woman from a palace window via a helicopter, as Marcelo had done. Both his siblings thought him rigid and stuck up. If he was, it was because he had to be. The path of his life had been laid out from his conception and he'd always known that to deviate from it could bring danger to his whole family. His siblings had not been so conscientious with their own recent behaviour. The pair of them had, in their differing ways, allowed their emotions to rule their heads and the repercussions had come close to threatening their family's existence. It had been left to him to clear up the mess of their making.

Marcelo's rumble of laughter at something his wife said echoed in Amadeo's ears as his gaze locked onto his sister stealing a kiss with her husband on the dance floor.

Draining his glass, he looked again at his blank-faced bride and his chest tightened. He would never be susceptible to the kind of adolescent emotions that had seen his siblings lose their heads but he'd hoped for more than this. More than a blank face from the despicable House of Fernandez.

Once the party had finished and her prince had thanked their guests, Elsbeth walked through the maze of wide corridors to their quarters. She'd been hugely looking forward to seeing the private space she and her husband would make their home. Tucked in an L on the ground floor of the castle, the size and proportions didn't disappoint. She followed Amadeo through a large reception room and into an even larger living area with high ceilings and an abundance of bay windows. Richly decorated in dusky pinks and gold, it surprised her how feminine their quarters were. The faint scent of paint told her it had been recently decorated.

'What do you think?' Amadeo asked her.

Knowing better than to tell the truth, she replied, 'It's beautiful.' She wouldn't dream of telling him she preferred bold colours and less kitschy furnishings, even if she didn't have the feeling it had been redecorated with her in mind.

He inclined his head and opened another door into a corridor. Instinct told her where this led and her heartbeat accelerated.

'The master bedroom,' he said blandly, opening the door at the far end.

What greeted her made Elsbeth, the cousin of a king, someone who'd lived her entire life in one of Europe's finest palaces, gasp.

Vast and high-ceilinged, most of the oakwood flooring was covered in a prettily patterned rug of pale blue threaded with gold. The four-poster bed was a work of art, the drapes pale blue damask, the headboard pale blue velvet topped with an elaborate gold moulded frieze of cherubs at play, at its foot a pale blue velvet chaise longue. The panelled walls were cream, the huge chandelier, along with all the other lighting, gold and crystal. This was a room fit for a queen, never mind a princess. Catching another trace of paint, she thought Amadeo must have stifled his own preferences to create a room with her in mind and, though he was wide of the mark with her taste, her heart swelled with gratitude that he'd gone to so much effort to make their home something he thought she would like and be comfortable in. It was a gesture that proved him a better man than the men in her family.

He indicated the two unobtrusive maids who'd followed them and said to Elsbeth, 'I shall take a shower in one of the guest bathrooms while you prepare for bed. I will join you when you are ready.'

She arranged her features into a smile, making sure to hide the relief that he wasn't going to remove the wedding dress himself. Another sign he was a gentleman! She knew perfectly well that Dominic had used her virginity as one of his selling points in the marriage negotiations. Men, Elsbeth had been assured, prized virginity in their brides.

Once the dress had been removed and carefully wrapped in tissue paper and boxed away, she sat at her antique dressing table having her hair brushed by a maid. There was something incredibly romantic about preparing herself for bed for the first time as a bride, she decided. The nightdress her mother had chosen for her, if not to Elsbeth's taste, was romantic too. White silk with thin straps, it was modestly cut, square beneath her collarbones and falling to mid-calf. Remembering the sage-green negligee she'd been drawn to, dismissed by her mother as being too 'slutty', she reminded herself of what her mother had said about this one being the perfect nightdress for a virgin giving herself to her husband. The virginal nightdress was very becoming and felt wonderful against her skin so she shouldn't complain, even if only to herself.

With her body and teeth clean, her face scrubbed of make-up and moisturised, her hair gleaming, the pretty virginal nightdress on and the bedsheets turned down, she was ready.

Swallowing the lump of fear that had suddenly formed in her throat, she smiled at the maids. 'You can leave me now. Please tell…' She swallowed again. 'Please tell the prince that he can join me.'

'Would you like the curtains of the bed to be drawn?' one of the maids asked.

Imagining with another clutch of fear how it would feel to be cocooned on the bed and only able to hear Amadeo's approach, she shook her head.

Alone, she took a deep breath and got under the bedsheets. After trying a number of positions, she ended up propping herself against the headboard, folded her hands loosely on her lap and, her heart thumping louder than ever, waited for her groom.

The wait seemed to take for ever. The longer it went on, the louder her mother's stern advice rang in her ears. *Wait for him to make the first move. Be compliant. Do whatever he tells you to do. Do not complain if it hurts.*

Give him a baby.

There was a knock on the door.

Taking one more deep breath, Elsbeth fixed a smile on her face and brightly called out, 'Come in.'

CHAPTER TWO

AMADEO'S GUTS CLENCHED as he crossed the threshold.

As he'd expected, his wind-up doll was waiting in the bed for him, expecting him to do his duty with that irritating vacuous smile on her face.

'Have I taken the right side of the bed?' she asked. 'I will move over if I've taken your side.'

It was the first time she'd instigated a conversation between them.

He shrugged his robe off and placed it on an antique armchair. 'It doesn't matter.'

Noticing the flush of colour on her cheeks at his nakedness, even though she avoided dipping her eyes any lower than his face, he climbed onto the bed and covered his lap with the bedsheets to spare her further blushes. Why Dominic had assumed the bride being a virgin made her a prized asset was beyond him. It just proved the sickness in Dominic's own head. Amadeo would be the first to agree that many traditions needed to be preserved to maintain royal mystique but the

concept of the virgin royal bride was something
he'd long believed consigned to the scrapbooks
of history.

He'd have preferred someone experienced.
Someone with a hint of nous and personality. But
Elsbeth had been offered, and Elsbeth had been a
willing pawn in the drive for peace between their
two nations.

They were both willing pawns, he thought
grimly. His own willingness stemmed only from
his desire to kill the existential threat to the Ceres
monarchy that a trade and diplomatic war with
Monte Cleure would bring. Elsbeth's willingness
came from her desire to be Queen.

God help him.

'Have you enjoyed our day?' he politely asked
to cut through the tension.

'Very much, thank you.'

'Anything you would have changed?'

'It was all perfect.'

'Even the coffee profiteroles?'

'They were delicious.'

'You ate little of yours.'

The vacuous smile dimmed a fraction. 'I'm
sorry.'

'Why?'

She blinked as if she didn't understand the
question.

Amadeo hid the fresh swell of irritation. 'You

have no need to apologise for disliking something.'

'I did like it,' she assured him, the smile firmly back in place.

Unsure why he wanted to argue this point, he let it go. He sensed Elsbeth would only agree with everything he said, so arguing would be fruitless.

It infuriated him that he even wanted to argue with her. A wedding night should not begin with the groom despising the bride and wanting to shout at her.

He had a job to do. Time to get on with it.

He turned his bedside light off and lay down.

'Would you like me to turn my light off too?' she asked.

'Unless you prefer to do it with the lights on?'

Her glimmer of uncertainty gave him a stab of guilt. His attempted humour had come out sounding more sarcastic than intended. Whatever his personal feelings towards her, Elsbeth was a virgin and likely to be nervous.

'You will probably feel more comfortable with the lights off,' he said in a gentler tone.

She turned her light off and copied him in lying down. The castle's ground lights were still on for their departing wedding guests, enough illumination filtering through the tiny gap in the heavy curtains for him to see she'd positioned herself on her back with her hands neatly folded on her belly.

Turning her face to him, she gave another smile.

It was the lack of emotion behind that smile that sent another wave of revulsion kicking through him. Sitting upright, he ran his fingers through his hair. 'I'm aware this is your first time.'

She didn't answer, just looked at him, her expression that of someone waiting for him to continue.

'You and I are strangers,' he said tersely. 'If you would rather we wait until we know each other better before we do this then all you have to do is say.' When she still didn't respond, he added in a tone he fought valiantly not to sound rough, 'Is this something you want to do?'

This time she spoke, and without any hesitation. 'Yes.'

Amadeo looked at her a moment longer. As pretty—as *beautiful*—as Elsbeth was, *he* didn't want to do this. Somehow he had to get this over and done with as quickly as he could, being as considerate and gentle as he could. Perfunctory sex. Close his eyes and think of Ceres.

Elsbeth's heart was beating so hard she could feel its impact against her ribs. She didn't know if it was anticipation of what was to come or fear that Amadeo might not go through with it.

If they didn't consummate their marriage, how could they make a baby? That terrified her far more than Amadeo's growing coldness towards her. Coldness and indifference she could deal with. Not having a baby and therefore always having the threat of being sent back to Monte Cleure hanging over her head… No. She didn't think she could handle that.

Should she hitch her nightdress up to her thighs and spread her legs to encourage him? Or would that be too wanton?

Too wanton, she decided. Her mother had been emphatic about it. Amadeo had to make the first move. Elsbeth was to be nothing but compliant putty in his hands.

And so she waited for him to make his move, doing nothing more than smile encouragement.

Her heart almost smashed through her ribs when he finally made his move and pulled the bedsheets off her.

His gaze drifted over her. If he liked what he saw, he gave no sign, but when he put his hands to hers and unfolded them from their position on her stomach there was a tenderness to his actions that loosened the knots in her belly she'd not even been aware had formed. Hovering over her, one hand splayed on the bed by her waist, his chiselled jaw tight, his chest rose before he lowered his face and kissed her.

In all Elsbeth's fantasies about their first kiss— the one at the cathedral didn't count as it had been only a dutiful peck on the lips—she'd imagined how it would feel. She'd imagined it would be warm and that it would feel nice. She'd certainly *hoped* it would feel nice if she was going to have to kiss him for the rest of her life. The last thing she'd expected was the crackle of electricity that shot through her.

This was more than *nice*…

Closing her eyes, she thrilled as the pressure of his mouth deepened and his hands began to roam over her body. Yes, this felt far, far more than nice, especially when he cupped her breast, and she squeezed her eyes tighter and reminded herself of her mother's words that she was only to be compliant. She must resist touching him back. If he wanted her to touch him, he would tell her. Amadeo was heir to a throne and, like all spouses of future kings, Elsbeth was his to command, nothing more.

For all her mother's words though, it was hard to stop herself shivering at the pleasure that came when he gathered the hem of her nightdress and tugged it up to her hips, his hand skimming the flesh of her inner thigh. Every brush of his skin against hers felt like fire. Delicious fire.

Amadeo had had enough. From his bride's unwillingness to touch him or respond properly to his kisses, he could believe that she too, was simply lying back and thinking of Ceres. Or, in her case, Monte Cleure. The only sign that she wasn't simply going through the motions came from the puckering of her nipples beneath the silk of her nightdress, but that could be easily explained by her being cold-blooded. Even when he traced his fingers up her thigh and over her soft, flat belly, she gave no reaction. It seemed his wind-up doll had run out of charge.

Ready to put an end to this travesty, he went to right himself and as he moved his hand away from the top of her thigh his fingers accidentally glanced between her legs. To his shock, he heard a faint mewing, the only sound of life since he'd kissed her.

He stared at Elsbeth for the longest time. Her chest was rising and falling rapidly, the finger and thumb of her left hand pinching and rubbing at the bedsheet.

Unsure if he was imagining this most silent display of desire, he tiptoed his fingers up her inner thigh and gently cupped her sex.

The last thing he expected to find there was heat.

The faint mew sounded again.

A bolt of lust suddenly crashed through him, as strong as he'd ever experienced, almost as if Elsbeth's heat had transfused through his skin and straight into his blood. Shocked at the strength of what he'd just experienced, it took a good few beats for Amadeo's head to clear.

His mouth now filled with moisture, his heart pumping hard, he gently ran his finger along the hot stickiness and was rewarded with a jerk of her body so subtle that, if he hadn't been paying such avid attention, it would have been imperceptible.

Slowly rubbing his finger over her swollen nub, he took in the closed eyes and trembling plump lips, the slight arching of her back and the tiny tremors shivering across her body.

Mio dio, she was as ripe for him as the juiciest plum.

All thoughts of climbing off the bed and leaving the room had gone. The erection that had gone from nothing to full bloom in less than a second throbbed, and he gripped it tightly to control the deepening ache.

Still keeping the pressure on her nub, he released his excitement and put his hand to her thigh. Gently, he spread it to one side. There was no resistance. All her fingers were now rubbing against the bedsheets.

Fascinated at her reactions, he pressed his knee to her other thigh but this time, her breaths now coming in short hitches, she parted it herself.

Not taking his eyes off her face, he carefully positioned himself between her legs, took back hold of his arousal and pressed it against her opening. Her eyes flickered but didn't open. The only sound was the scratching of her fingers against the mattress.

Moving slowly, he inched himself inside her. When he clenched his jaw, it wasn't through irritation but for control because, *dio*, he'd never, in his whole life, felt such welcoming heat. So exquisite did it feel that he had to grit his teeth and remind himself that Elsbeth was a virgin. With infinite care, he slowly buried himself all the way inside her.

And then he felt the lightest of touches as finally...*finally*...she touched him. Her hand on his back was so light he probably would not have noticed had his skin not burned beneath it.

Gripping tightly to the sides of the pillow her beautiful head rested on, Amadeo closed his eyes and began to move. *Mio Dio...*

Elsbeth had never in her wildest dreams imagined it could be like this. Could feel like this. She'd expected pain at worst, discomfort at best. She hadn't expected pleasure. Pleasure was something she'd hoped for once she'd become accustomed to sex. But *this*...oh, it was incredible. She'd never known anything like it, and as Amadeo's strong body moved over hers, steadily increasing the tempo of his thrusts, little grunts of pleasure vibrated from his throat and something deep in the heart of her began to pulse strongly and thicken.

Never had Amadeo fought to hold back his release as he did in that moment. The exquisite pain of this self-torture was more than he'd thought himself capable of enduring but still he fought, refusing to let go and fall into the indulgence of the ultimate pleasure, not until...

And then he sensed it happening. It was there in the shortening of her quiet breaths and the tightening around his arousal. Overcome by the sudden urgent need to look at her, he raised himself onto his elbows at the same moment Elsbeth's eyes flew wide open in glazed shock and locked onto his, and her lips parted in a silent O.

He could hold on no more. Burying himself as deep inside her as was humanly possible, Amadeo let go.

Elsbeth tried valiantly to pull herself back to earth and knit herself back together. It felt as if she'd been shattered into stardust. She could hardly breathe through the heavy beats of her heart.

That had been...

Nothing came to her. No single word could describe what she'd just experienced. She'd had no idea. No idea it could feel like that. Not for her.

Her mother had been wrong.

Amadeo's cheek, pressed so tightly against hers, turned aside. He pulled away from her and rolled onto his back.

Feeling the cold of his loss, she swallowed to stop herself crying out a protest.

Had he liked what they'd done as much as she had? She wished she could ask. As with so many things in her life, this was a wish she dared not grant herself.

Amadeo had never known silence could be so loud. The thrills of his climax still laced his blood but the whooshing in his head had finally lessened enough for him to think. His thoughts though, gave no comfort.

The last thing he'd expected was to enjoy sex with his new wife, although 'enjoy' was the wrong word. It didn't fit at all. But then, neither did any other word.

He supposed he should take solace that his weekly duty wouldn't be the chore he'd envisaged.

Closing his eyes first to brace himself, he turned his stare back to her.

Her eyes were open.

'Elsbeth?' he said quietly.

He watched as she summoned the vacuous smile as she turned to face him.

'Are you okay?' he asked.

'Yes.'

Unable to read anything other than emptiness behind the returning stare, he breathed deeply and nodded. 'That's good.' He climbed off the bed and strode over to his discarded robe. 'Do you know how to contact the domestic staff if you need them?'

'Yes.'

He inclined his head again as he put his arms in his robe. 'Good. Then I will leave you to get some sleep.'

Her head lifted sharply. 'You're...?' But she snapped her mouth shut before she'd finished uttering her first word.

'You're?' he prompted.

The smile returned. She shook her head. 'Nothing.'

Staring at her, he tried to decipher the flash of emotion he'd detected when she'd opened her mouth. 'Tell me what you were going to say.'

Her throat moved and her lips pulled in together before she answered. 'I was just going to ask where you'll be sleeping.'

Still watching her closely, he tightened the belt of his robe. 'I thought you were aware of our living arrangements. They were agreed during the negotiations.' When she only continued staring at him, he smothered a sigh. 'Were you told about the arrangements?'

There was a slight hesitation before she shook her head. 'No.'

'You should have been. I was told you were in agreement with them.'

'I will abide with whatever has been agreed between you and my cousin,' she intoned.

Was she for real? She couldn't be. If he couldn't still feel the imprint of her body on his skin, he would question if she was even human.

'These are your quarters. I have separate ones on the floor above.' At her blank expression, he only just stopped himself from adding, *Nod if you understand what I just said.* Instead, he continued with, 'We will see a great deal of each other during our shared engagements but our private lives will be separate. I've been told you are keen to be a mother—is that correct?'

Her nod was emphatic. 'Yes.'

'Good. Then I suggest we share a bed together each Saturday until a child is conceived. Do you agree?'

The vacuous smile this time came complete with pretty, white, even teeth. 'I will abide with whatever you think best.'

'I do think that is best.'

'Then I abide.'

Needing to get out of this room and far away from the woman he'd married before he said something he'd live to regret, Amadeo bowed his head. 'Then I wish you a goodnight.'

'Goodnight,' she replied.

After closing the bedroom door behind him, Amadeo took what felt like the deepest breath of his life.

He really had married a wind-up doll. Beneath the beautiful veneer, there was nothing. Only emptiness.

Elsbeth pulled the bedsheets up to her neck, closed her eyes and swallowed to get air into her lungs.

Why had her mother not warned her that she would be living alone in this castle? She must have known. Her mother knew everything. She had a way of listening at doors. Elsbeth had tried it herself once but had been caught. The beating she'd received from her father had stopped her ever trying the same again. Mercifully, it was the only beating she'd ever suffered, but it was a lesson she'd never forgotten and never wished to have repeated.

It was inconceivable that her mother hadn't known. It wouldn't have changed her mind about marrying Amadeo. Nothing could have changed her mind. The opportunity to escape Monte Cleure had been too great.

A royal woman's role was as an adornment, her function to breed and obey. Elsbeth knew that. She'd seen it and lived it every day of her life, and she knew she should be grateful that living separately from Amadeo made it much less likely that she could disappoint him. Much less likely that she'd find herself on the receiving end of his displeasure. Much less likely she would find out what form of chastisement his displeasure took. Her gut told her he would not be a man to use his hands as weapons for punishment, but powerful men didn't need to use their hands to punish women. There were a myriad of ways they could punish them, and she had no idea what form Amadeo's punishments would take.

Whatever form his punishments ended up taking—and it was a near certainty, whatever their living arrangements, that one day she *would* do something to displease him—what kind of fool would she be to listen to her gut? Hadn't it tantalised her with the possibility of happiness in her new country with her new husband?

The solitary tear rolling down her cheek told her happiness was as far away as it had ever been.

CHAPTER THREE

Elsbeth lay under Amadeo's weight, his breathing heavy in her ear.

Their second copulation. She wouldn't call it making love. Couldn't call it that. It was humiliating that she'd enjoyed it so much. More humiliating that she longed to wrap her arms tightly around him and press her mouth and nose into his strong neck and breathe him in. She supposed it was the euphoria of good sex bringing those longings out in her. It certainly wasn't him.

Their 'honeymoon week' had been spent apart. Elsbeth had spent it with only her domestic staff for company. She'd dined alone. She'd had no visitors. Her husband's absence had been stark.

Amadeo shifted his weight off her. Immediately she conjured her smile. She doubted he'd see it but she was taking no chances. A royal woman must always be agreeable. Or face the consequences.

No, she didn't think he'd notice whether she smiled or not because the room was in complete darkness. There had been a slight gap in the curtains of the window nearest the bed but he'd closed it himself before getting into bed beside her, turning off the lights and getting down to business. From the moment he'd entered her room that evening and made some stilted effort at small talk, his eyes had rested on her face for barely seconds at a time.

Despite all her best efforts to please him and be agreeable, Amadeo did not want to be married to her. She knew it in her heart.

When he wished her a goodnight a short while later, it took everything she had to wish him the same in her usual bright tone.

Please, please let me conceive soon.

Another lonely week passed, ending with Elsbeth sitting at her dressing table while the castle's beauty team transformed her appearance for her first Saturday evening engagement, which was being held at the Italian embassy, in her honour no less.

She'd undertaken only four engagements that week with Amadeo. They had been select daytime engagements with Ceresian industry, chosen to ease her into her new role as princess. Having often acted as Dominic's consort since he'd inherited the throne, she'd found the familiar routine soothing and a welcome distraction from her loneliness.

For the first time, she felt an unexpected pang

of homesickness. At least she'd had friends in Monte Cleure, cousins and second cousins she'd been raised and educated with. She knew exactly where in the palace she was permitted, knew who to trust—no one—and who to be extra wary of. She'd had her mother to guide her. She missed her wise counsel. She missed having a goodnight kiss brushed against her cheek each evening. Her new family in Ceres, she feared, had already forgotten her existence.

She felt guilt that, despite all her mother's coaching and advice, Elsbeth had turned her husband away from her. All their engagements were shared but they had been as lonely as if she'd conducted them alone. Amadeo's Prince Charming persona did not extend to her. In public he was courteous and gentlemanly and stayed close to her side like a good prince should, and yet somehow he managed to avoid ever touching her. All journeys to and from their engagements were spent in the back of their car with their private secretaries and security, all conversation conducted in rapid Italian. Elsbeth understood Italian but not at the speed in which they spoke it. It only served to exacerbate her sense of isolation.

With the time rapidly approaching for their latest engagement, one that would end with Amadeo sharing her bed for a short while, Elsbeth tried to cheer herself up. Loneliness was making her wear rose-coloured glasses about Monte Cleure. Here, in Ceres, she had more freedom than she'd ever enjoyed. If her staff were spying on her, they hid it well. She was allowed to choose the food she ate and the clothes she wore. She'd not once inwardly cowered under menaces or threats…

But, as she thought the latter, she became aware of a dull ache deep in her abdomen that quickly turned into a painful cramp. As a beautician was, at that moment, sweeping her eyelashes with mascara, Elsbeth fought the instinct to double over, instead clenching her teeth and gripping tightly to the arms of the chair she was sitting in, and rode out the pain.

Amadeo, having just had a scotch poured for him and bracing himself for the evening ahead, was surprised at his brother's appearance in his quarters. 'I'm about to leave for the embassy,' he told him.

'I know. I wanted to catch you before you left.'

'Is something wrong?' Their quarters were reasonably close together but generally they found it easier to message or call when they wanted something from the other.

Marcelo helped himself to a scotch. 'Clara's been badgering me to arrange a night for you and Elsbeth to have dinner with us.'

'For what purpose?'

His brother leaned back against the mahogany bar. Where Elsbeth's quarters had been turned into a princess's paradise, Amadeo's own identically sized quarters had a dark gothic vibe. His mean-spirited misanthrope grandmother had lived in the quarters before him, and most of the dark wood furnishings and intense chiaroscuro paintings from artists such as Caravaggio had been there since her time. As the only thing he required from his quarters was privacy, he'd seen no need to make many changes to it.

'For the purpose that she's the newest member of our family and we've seen nothing of her since the wedding,' Marcelo replied. 'Clara's been itching to spend time with her and I'm afraid I can't restrain her any more—she says two weeks is long enough for the two of you to spend alone getting to know each other, so unless you agree and set a date you'll have Clara to deal with.'

This was the most effective threat Marcelo could have hit him with. Knowing better than to roll his eyes—Marcelo was extremely protective of his wife and Amadeo had no wish for another punch in the stomach—he inclined his head. 'I'm sure something can be arranged.'

And something arranged could be unarranged. He had no desire to suffer Elsbeth's perma-vacuous smile aimed at him over a dinner table unnecessarily for a whole evening. It was always there. Always. His wife must have the strongest cheek muscles in the universe.

'Where is she?' Marcelo craned his neck as if he expected her to emerge from the walls.

'Either in her quarters or waiting for me in our joint reception room, so unless you want me to be late meeting her and then late for our engagement I—'.

'Why isn't she here with you?'

'She has her own quarters.'

The silence that followed this wouldn't normally bother him but, coming from Marcelo, it was unusual. 'What?'

His brother narrowed his eyes. 'How much time have you spent with her since the wedding?'

'Enough.' More than enough.

'How much? Clara overheard one of the domestic staff saying you and Elsbeth are leading completely separate lives.'

'I hope she reprimanded the staff member for spreading gossip,' Amadeo said sharply.

His brother grunted a laugh. 'Clara reprimand anyone?'

He grunted a laugh back. As soon as he'd realised how unsuited Clara was to being a royal princess, Amadeo had done a U-turn and worked to prevent Marcelo's marriage to her, believing the damage she could do with her unfiltered, unthinking ways was too great to risk. He'd been proved wrong—the public loved her and, if he was being truthful with himself, he was growing to love her too—but not *that* wrong as it had been his idea and insistence that they marry in the first place. All the same, he often found himself biting his tongue when she was overfamiliar with the staff or shared indiscreet stories that had no place at a royal dinner table. He could easily imagine her overhearing talk and gleefully demanding to know more.

Now he understood why Marcelo had come to his quarters rather than just call him.

'I had to tell her this was just a spiteful rumour and that you wouldn't be so callous as to treat your new wife so shabbily,' Marcelo added.

'What is shabby about it?' he asked tightly. 'She is living in quarters that have been made fit for a queen, with everything she could want or need at her disposal. She wants for nothing.'

'So it is true?'

'It is no more and no less than was agreed in the terms of our marriage.' Terms he'd been upfront about with his family and with the King of Monte Cleure. That Dominic and his advisors hadn't seen fit to tell Elsbeth about it was regrettable but, once he'd advised her of their living arrangements himself, she'd been perfectly agreeable—when *wasn't* she agreeable?—to it. *Dio*, if she was any more sweet and agreeable she'd come coated in fondant icing.

Marcelo's face darkened. 'You see nothing of her?'

'We conduct our engagements together.'

'And that is it?' He shook his head in blatant disbelief. 'Clara and Alessia are desperate to get to know her and invite her out with them but Gabriel and I told them to give you a few weeks to get to know each other and settle into your marriage, and all this time she's been alone in her quarters? How can you treat her in this way?'

'Need I remind you that I married a Fernandez to save our country and our monarchy from a situation *you* ignited? A *Fernandez*.' He practically spat the word out. 'I do my duty by her and I do and say nothing disrespectful to her. Elsbeth wants for nothing.'

'We all hate her family,' Marcelo snapped. 'Her cousin kidnapped my wife. If anyone should hate her for her blood it's Clara, but she wants to give her a chance and befriend her. Elsbeth is a young woman alone in a strange country. You're her husband. Whatever reason you took those vows, you did take them, and you owe it to her to give her a chance. I'm not saying you have to live with her, but she deserves *something*. She might one day be the mother of your children…if the rumours are right that you have graced her with your royal presence in the bedroom on two separate occasions?'

'Your wife certainly knows how to extract idle gossip,' he snapped back. It infuriated him that his brother, whose undignified bout of rule-breaking had cast the stone creating ripples that had led to Amadeo having to marry Elsbeth, should cast judgement on him. 'For your information, Elsbeth is perfectly happy with our living arrangements. I do not interfere with your marriage and I will not tolerate you interfering with mine, so let us regard your lecture as over. You can see yourself out—I have an engagement to attend.'

Downing the last of his scotch, he slammed the crystal glass on top of his three-hundred-year-old piano and stalked out of his quarters.

Amadeo usually enjoyed his time at the Italian embassy. Sharing a language and much of the same culture made the two nations natural allies, and time spent with the gregarious ambassador was rarely a chore. This evening's engagement was far different to normal, as all his engagements that week had been. Used to working a crowd and meeting dignitaries on his own, having a companion who wasn't a blood member of his family put a different flavour on events.

The few engagements he'd shared with his wife that week had been designed to ease her into her new role. She'd handled them with aplomb. In truth, it would have been impossible for her to put a foot wrong considering she stuck to his side like glue, smiled vacuously and let him do all the talking.

But those had been business engagements. To-night's embassy gathering was a social event in

Elsbeth's honour and, as their first course was being cleared away, she was still to open her mouth for anything other than food.

Biting back his irritation, he leaned into her and whispered, 'I think the ambassador's husband is feeling overwhelmed to be sitting next to you. Why don't you talk to him and put him at ease?'

She blinked slowly, widened her smile and turned to the man in question. Her voice was too low for him to hear what she said but the ambassador's husband responded. Soon the two of them were deep in conversation...or, rather, the husband was deep in conversation, Elsbeth deep in listening. When the ambassador excused herself for a few minutes, Amadeo turned his full attention to them. Elsbeth's head was turned away from him but she must have sensed he wished to join in for she adjusted her stance so the conversation could include him too. The husband, it transpired, was telling Elsbeth all about the school his children went to.

'What subjects do they find the most interesting?' she asked when he came up for air, which immediately set him off again.

When the ambassador returned to her seat, it struck Amadeo that Elsbeth had so skilfully woven the conversation so that it was all about him, and given him the full weight of her attention, that the ambassador's husband had hardly registered Amadeo's presence.

Unsure why this should irk him, Amadeo threw himself back into conversation with the ambassador but when, much later, their coffee cups were being cleared away and everyone in attendance had followed his lead and risen to their feet, he found he still had one ear on Elsbeth and the husband, paying enough attention that both ears strained when he heard the husband say, 'Are you okay, Your Highness?'

He had to strain even harder to hear her reply and, as she spoke, he realised Elsbeth always pitched her voice so that it was just audible. 'I'm fine, thank you.'

'Are you sure? You've gone very pale.'

Turning sharply to look at his wife, he saw what the other man meant. The subtle blush on Elsbeth's pretty cheekbones visibly contrasted with the paleness of her usually golden complexion.

'I thank you for caring, but I promise you I am well and would very much like to see Livia's painting.'

The ambassador caught Amadeo's eye and murmured with an indulgent eye-roll, 'Giuseppe thinks our eldest daughter is going to be the next Frida Kahlo.'

As the CEO of Italy's biggest car manufacturer

was heading towards him, Amadeo was forced to stay where he was and not follow his wife.

It disturbed him that he wanted to follow her at all.

Amadeo's private secretary and head of security kept up the usual flow of chatter on the drive home. Amadeo joined in as he always did but Elsbeth was aware of him glancing across at her face far more than he usually did, and didn't dare let her smile drop for a second.

Rather than scare herself by imagining his reaction to what she needed to tell him when they reached her quarters, Elsbeth thought longingly of a hot bath and a large glass of port to help ease her cramping stomach.

Nothing was said between them from the car all the way to her quarters. Every step though, increased the rate of her heart.

All evening she'd been worrying about the news she'd have to share with him, so much so that Amadeo had felt the need to tell her to make conversation with Giuseppe because her head had been too full of worry to engage with him. Poor Giuseppe. And he was such a nice man too. She hoped she'd made up for her initial rudeness.

Her two evening maids appeared moments after they entered her quarters.

'The princess won't be needing your assistance this evening.' Amadeo's smoothly delivered words made her stomach plunge. 'Feel free to return to your rooms—she will call if she needs you.'

Instead of obeying, they both looked at Elsbeth. To her horror, she realised they were waiting for her to give *her* assent.

Locking eyes with Amadeo, she caught what could only be described as annoyance as his look quite clearly said, *Go on then, dismiss them.*

'I'll call you if I need anything,' she said with a smile which hurt her cheeks.

They both nodded. 'Goodnight, Your Highness.'

'Goodnight.'

She couldn't help closing her eyes when the door closed and, for the first time in a week, she was alone with her husband.

Panic clutched at her chest.

Why had he dismissed the maids? Was he angry with her about something? She thought quickly, frantically, wondering what faux pas she could have made that evening. The only thing she could think of was his having to tell her to make conversation with Giuseppe. Would something that innocuous be enough to aggravate him? She wished she knew. Two weeks into their marriage and her husband was still a stranger to her.

'Would you like a drink?' he surprised her by asking.

She took a deep breath to stem the panic and get a grip of herself. The following conversation was not going to be easy and working herself into a lather about an unknown quantity would not help. That she had to admit to failure in their quest for conception was enough to worry about. She'd take whatever else he wanted to throw at her as it came. 'Yes, please.'

Amadeo rifled through her bar. Not knowing what Elsbeth liked to drink, he'd ordered it to be stocked with every kind of alcoholic and soft drink. It didn't surprise him to find not a single bottle had been touched.

Helping himself to a fifteen-year-old scotch, he poured a liberal amount, took a gulp of it then turned back to her and raised the bottle in a question.

She shook her head. Her smile didn't seem as wide as she usually fixed it, he noted.

'What would you prefer? Wine? Champagne? Something stronger?'

'Is there any port?'

Anyone would think it was his bar and not hers. 'There is everything.'

'Then I would like a glass of port. Please.'

He found the bottle easily enough, poured her a hefty measure, then topped up his scotch. From the corner of his eye he noticed her press a hand low into her abdomen and her shoulders rise as if she were sucking in a breath.

Carrying the glasses over to her, he held her port out.

'Sit down, Elsbeth,' he said as she took her drink from him with quiet thanks.

Just as he knew she would, she obeyed, sitting primly on an armchair with dusky pink upholstery.

Choosing the Chesterfield for himself, he took another sip of his scotch before saying, 'You don't look well. What's wrong with you?'

She closed her eyes and breathed in as if bracing herself, then whispered, 'Menstrual pains.'

'Have you been in pain all evening?'

Her gaze fixed on floor, she nodded.

'I thought something was wrong when Giuseppe commented that you looked unwell. Why didn't you tell me before we left?'

'I was embarrassed to tell you in front of other people.' She breathed in deeply again. 'I'm sorry.'

'Sorry for what?' he asked, faintly bemused.

'That I've failed to conceive.'

What on *earth*...?

'Elsbeth, look at me.'

She raised her head slowly. For the first time he saw real human emotion on the usually empty expression. The expression was one of fear.

CHAPTER FOUR

ELSBETH CLASPED HER trembling hands tightly around the glass, her mind awhirl. Was this the reason Amadeo had dismissed her maids? Because he'd realised she was feeling unwell? That suggested a degree of empathy, didn't it? Which was a good thing. Even so, would that empathy extend to her failing at the first attempt to conceive a child? Amidst these thoughts her mother's voice echoed, stressing the importance of conceiving as soon as possible, stressing that royal men would not take the failure to conceive as their own failure, stressing that menstruation itself disgusted them.

She tried not to flinch when Amadeo leaned forwards and rested his elbows on his lap.

Swirling the amber liquid in his glass, his narrowed eyes didn't leave her face. And then he tipped his drink down his throat, wiped the residue off his lips with his thumb and said, 'What are you frightened of?'

Elsbeth took a sip of her port. The almost sweet

liquid slid down her throat and injected her with strength. 'Disappointing you.'

'And you think I'm disappointed that you're not pregnant even though we've only been married for two weeks?'

'I would not want to disappoint you in any way.' She forced herself to ask, 'Are you disappointed with me?'

He grimaced and closed his eyes. 'Not in the way you think.'

Her heart sank heavily and she breathed out a sigh. 'Oh.'

He fixed his stare back on her. 'My disappointment is not your fault, Elsbeth.'

She could only gaze at him, trying to read the expression in his clear green eyes, grateful that for once she didn't see irritation in them.

And then he opened his mouth and she wished for the irritation to come back.

'You're not the kind of woman I envisaged making my queen.'

Her throat caught at the starkly delivered admission.

'Given a choice, I would never have married a Fernandez.' His thumb played on the rim of his glass. 'I despise your family. But that is not your fault,' he reiterated, and Elsbeth wondered if he could hear how grudging that reiteration sounded. She realised with a stab of despair that he wanted it to be her fault. He *wanted* to hate her.

She summoned all her skills to stop the hurt showing on her face. Amadeo's attitude to her family shouldn't come as a surprise; she despised them too, and she had to fight equally hard to smother the urge to shout that she was nothing like the others, that she couldn't help the blood that ran in her veins and that he should judge her for *her* and not be influenced by his preconceived notions about her.

She would never say any of it, of course. She wouldn't argue with him even if she hadn't spent her life witnessing the consequences for royal women who dared argue with their husbands or fathers: the thickly applied concealer that didn't quite hide the bruised skin beneath, the stiffness in their stride.

While she still believed Amadeo was not a man to use his hands to instil obedience in his wife, her position as his wife was so precarious that she didn't need to give him more ammunition with which to hate her.

The simple truth that trumped everything else was that she'd rather be married to a man who hated her than return to Monte Cleure.

And at least she knew. She wouldn't have to spend the rest of her life, or however long her marriage lasted, wondering why she felt such coldness from her husband. Her very existence made him cold.

For as long as she remained childless, her po-

sition as his wife would never be safe. But she'd
known that already.

'I want to assure you that my personal feelings
towards your family do not mean I will treat you
with anything other than respect,' he said into the
silence. 'I know it will take time but I want us to
have a good relationship. It will make life easier
for us both.'

She conjured her smile back into place. 'I feel
the same.'

'Good.' He drained his scotch. 'Are you happy
with our living arrangements?'

'Yes.' That was only a partial lie. Despite the
loneliness, she'd come to quite like having a home
to call her own and being able to relax in it. These
quarters were hers in a way nothing had ever belonged to her before.

'My brother thinks I've effectively abandoned
you. Do you agree with him?'

'Our living arrangements were agreed before
our marriage.'

'That's not an answer.' Rubbing the back of his
neck, his shoulders rose. 'If there's anything that
makes you unhappy, you must tell me. I cannot
read minds, and my sister would be the first person to tell you that I cannot read women.'

Amadeo's effort at humour brought no response. 'Are you unhappy?' he pressed.

'No.'

Truth or lie? He didn't know her well enough

to be sure. He didn't know her at all. The brief flare of emotion—*had* it been fear?—he'd seen in her eyes had been shuttered behind the usual vacuity with such speed that he wondered if he'd imagined it. If his honesty had affected her, she'd done a wonderful job in hiding it, holding his stare without looking away, movement in those baby blue eyes but nothing to read in them.

'Are you happy with your quarters?'

'Yes.' The emphasis she put in this affirmation rang true.

'And are you content with your life here?'

She was equally emphatic. 'Yes.'

Damn Marcelo for planting ideas in his head. His brother had palpitations when he spent more than five minutes apart from Clara, but that was because his brother was 'in love' and ruled by hormones and emotion. Marcelo couldn't appreciate just how different Amadeo and Elsbeth's marriage was, that in essence it was one of convenience. Even if Amadeo had married a woman he actually liked, his marriage would still have been in a similar vein. It was usual for royalty to have separate bedrooms if not separate quarters. His siblings were the anomaly in that.

All the same, Amadeo could appreciate that his brother might have a point about Elsbeth being lonely.

'We have a full schedule of engagements this week.' Elsbeth's easing-in period was over. From now on their itineraries meant their weekdays and a couple of evenings each week would be spent together. Chances were Elsbeth would be as sick of the sight of him as he would be of her and relish the evenings and weekend days spent apart. 'Are you going to be well enough to do them?'

Dark colour stained her previously pale cheeks. 'I'll be fine by Monday. The pains normally only last a day.'

'Have you taken anything for it?'

She raised her glass and gave a wry smile. It was the first smile from her that didn't revolt him.

He rubbed his neck again. 'If I'd known you were unwell, I would have cancelled our engagement.'

'It's just cramps,' she said quickly. 'I was fine. There is no need to cancel anything on my behalf.'

'Have you seen a doctor about it?'

Her cheeks turned so dark he had the impression she was on the verge of spontaneously combusting with embarrassment. 'It's only menstrual cramps.'

'I'll get Dr Jessop to see you. He's my mother and sister's gynaecologist.' Pulling his phone out of his inside pocket, he called his private secretary.

When he was done, Elsbeth was staring at him

in wary shock. 'Are you getting the doctor to see me *now*?'

'It would be rather pointless having him see you when you are well,' he riposted drily, then nodded at the glass in her hand. 'Another drink while we wait?'

He caught a flash of gratitude in her eyes, her smile soft. 'Yes, please. And thank you. It's very kind of you to bring the doctor to me.'

His chest tightened in a way he'd never felt before. After a beat, he said, 'Don't ever feel you have to suffer in silence.'

Two days later, Elsbeth hit the ground running with her first full week of engagements. Their teams—hers and Amadeo's—had arranged timings for maximum efficiency, the royal couple and their entourage moving from one engagement to the next with fluid precision. Her first proper evening engagement came on her first day too, an award ceremony for Ceres' most successful and innovative young entrepreneurs. She was given an exact two-hour window at the castle to prepare herself. Her beauty team were waiting for her and sprang straight into action. As a result, she and Amadeo arrived at the awards venue at the exact appointed time.

After posing for the press photographers, they were taken straight to their table for the preceding four-course meal.

Now knowing what was expected of her, Elsbeth turned to the gentleman on her right, the event organiser, who also happened to be Ceres' youngest billionaire, and struck up a conversation.

As fascinating as the man was on paper though, she found herself having to concentrate hard on their talk, every inch of her painfully attuned to the man sitting on her right. Amadeo.

Had she imagined that he'd made an effort to include her more that day in the conversations that flowed with their private secretaries? That he'd slowed his speech so she could keep up more easily? It was hard to be certain, it could have just been a necessity for him because of the sheer size of their workload. It didn't help that she was so *aware* of him, of his languid movements, the bronzed flesh of his throat above his starched white collar and tie, the surprising elegance of his huge hands... And now she was having to contend with all that awareness of him while he was wrapped in a tuxedo. Was it any wonder she was in danger of her brain scrambling?

What was it about the wearing of a tuxedo that magnified a man's masculinity? On the drive to the event she'd had to fight harder than normal not to stare at him.

Their first course was cleared away. Having come to a natural pause in her chat with the organiser, Elsbeth had a sip of her wine, then found herself holding her breath as Amadeo leaned his body a little closer to hers—not close enough that he brushed against her but close enough for her awareness to rocket—and said in an undertone for her ears only, 'How are you feeling now? Have your pains gone?'

The barest whisper of his breath caught in her hair. A frisson raced up her spine...and down too, into the apex of her thighs. Stunned at such an instantaneous reaction, Elsbeth had to force her body into stillness. Arranging a smile on her face, she met his stare. 'Much better, thank you.'

'I thought you looked better.' A fleeting wry smile played on his lips. 'But I am aware of the tricks women can use with make-up to make themselves appear healthier than they are. Alessia is an expert at it.'

It was the sensuality in the firm lips as he spoke that finally scrambled Elsbeth's brain. For too long a moment, all she could do was keep her smile fixed in place while she strove desperately for a response. 'Thank you again for calling the doctor to me.'

He inclined his head. 'I'm glad he was able to help you. You stored his number in your phone so you can call him directly if you need him?'

'Yes. Thank you.'

His green eyes continued to bore into hers as if he was searching for something or waiting for something, but then the evening's servers

swarmed to their table with their second course
and whatever Amadeo was searching for or waiting for was forgotten.

Elsbeth arranged herself on the bed and tried to
breathe through the tightness in her lungs, her
ears straining for the sound of Amadeo's arrival
in her quarters.

The effort she'd sensed him making on Monday
had continued throughout the week. There had
been a definite shift in his attitude towards her.
He included her more, especially during conversations when they were being ferried backwards
and forwards to engagements. She tried hard to
reciprocate, working harder than ever to maintain
her agreeable persona and be the most perfect
adornment a future king could wish for.

But he still made sure to never touch her, still
wished her a goodnight from the reception room
that connected their individual quarters and then
disappeared up his private stairs without so much
as the suggestion of a drink together. She still
hadn't been invited into his quarters. She had no
idea what he got up to in the privacy of his own
domain, but the shift in his attitude made her
hopeful that one day soon she would be invited
into it. Maybe one night she would be invited to
share *his* bed.

A pulse burned between her legs and she
squeezed her eyes tightly shut, trying to tamp

down the thrills of anticipation spreading along her veins.

And then she heard movement and her heart set off into a canter.

Amadeo assumed that going without sex for two weeks was the reason he didn't dread joining Elsbeth that night, and the reason he descended the stairs to her quarters with his heart and loins thrumming.

But they'd thrummed since he'd woken.

Anticipation was understandable, he reasoned. The three weeks of his marriage had resulted in the least amount of sex that he'd had since his teenage years... Not quite true, he reminded himself. He'd called off the casual relationship he'd been in as soon as his marriage to Elsbeth had been agreed. The six weeks of celibacy from then until the wedding had been perfectly manageable. Amadeo had a high sex drive but his position meant it was something he'd always had to manage. In his adult life a series of discreet affairs with like-minded rich women—rich women had no need to sell stories about him—had sated his appetites as much as they could. There had been occasions when he'd wondered if he'd be fortunate enough to find a suitable wife with a matching drive for sex but, with all the other attributes that had to come above it, had not held his breath. Self-denial was nothing new to him, had been an underlying factor of his whole life. He'd known since he could form thoughts that he was heir to the throne of a great and noble country and that his behaviour and the choices he made must always reflect that. Personal desires were an unwanted inconvenience, something his siblings would have done well to remember.

Elsbeth's head of housekeeping let him in. The other domestic staff had already been dismissed for the night.

His veins thickening, he walked along the corridor to her bedroom.

As expected, she was waiting in bed for him, propped upright against the velvet headboard wearing another variation of sacrificial virgin nightdress. The vacuous smile that turned his stomach was firmly in place.

He'd left her quarters a week ago thinking they'd reached an *entente cordiale*. He would make more of an effort with her, he'd vowed, but *dio*, it was hard, especially as Elsbeth had slipped back into her wind-up doll ways. He'd noticed though, that when they were on engagements she'd become more engaged with the people they met, more willing to share a few words and show her interest. She'd positively charmed the event organiser on Monday evening, had him eating out of her hand. It was just when it came to Amadeo alone that she reverted to being vacuously smiley. Elsbeth still answered his questions in few words and never volunteered anything about herself. If he didn't make the effort of conversation there would be no conversation at all. He supposed the constant smiles stopped her talking much. Getting cheek muscles and lips to multitask was a difficult ask. Or maybe he was being too generous and his initial impression had been right—there wasn't enough going on in her head for her to hold a conversation.

'How has your day been?' he asked as he removed his robe.

A blush stained her cheeks and she averted her eyes from his body without losing the brightness of her expression. 'Fine, thank you.'

'What have you done with yourself?'

'I went for a walk with Clara and her dogs.'

At least that had saved his almost monosyllabic wife from having to talk. Clara could talk for the whole of Europe.

He slid under the covers. 'Do you like her company?'

'Very much.'

Effusive praise indeed, coming from his wife.

'And you?' she asked after a small hesitation. 'Have you had a good day?'

'I spent it at the Ceres National Racetrack. I'm an investor in a racing team who were testing there. Sébastien, the team principal, is an old friend of mine. I went along to watch and had dinner with him and one of the drivers.'

Elsbeth, struggling to breathe as the heat from Amadeo's body and the scent emanating from him seeped into her senses, scrambled for something else to say. She settled on, 'You are a fan of motor racing?' and then inwardly cringed at how gauche she must sound. But this was what Amadeo did to her. Overwhelmed her.

Life had taught her to be cautious and always think before she did or said anything, but it was a trait that amplified around him. When he was this close to her, her brain turned to mush. That he was naked and close enough that all she needed to do was move her foot a few inches and it would brush against his skin, made every cell in her body stand on end and every nerve strain towards him. The anticipation of Amadeo making his move and twisting his body to lean into her was almost unbearable.

'Obviously or I wouldn't invest in it,' he said.

Amidst the inward cringing and thrumming awareness sparked a tiny thread of anger, and she had to fight hard to keep her expression amiable and her tone bright. 'That's good.'

She didn't even know what she meant by that. *That's good.* What was good? That he had an interest in something outside the royal family? That he'd escaped the castle for the day?

She widened her smile, not making any motion that could betray her accelerating bitterness at his failure to mention in all the time they'd spent together that week that he was going off on a private jaunt.

He hadn't mentioned it because then he might have felt compelled to ask her along too.

Lying alone in her bed an hour later, Elsbeth stared up at the tester. Despite the lingering tingles racing through her body, only emptiness lay in the place where her heart should be, and she placed a hand to her chest to check it was still beating. It pulsed strongly against her palm and with it came a swell of tears to know that sex with her was nothing but a chore for him. Amadeo knew exactly what to do to make it good for her but never went beyond that. He made no attempt to see her naked and never kissed her anywhere but her mouth. He didn't invite her to touch or kiss him anywhere.

Maybe it was for the best that he always left straight after they were done. That he always made her climax… that was the problem. It softened her, weakened her limbs and lowered her emotional defences.

Made her ache for a tenderness that could never be hers.

Elsbeth added a sweep of mascara to her eyelashes.

Another week had passed.

Her life had turned into Groundhog Week.

Monday to Friday engagements, weekends and non-engagement evenings spent apart from her husband…

Apart from Duty Night. She'd taken to calling it that because she knew that was how Amadeo viewed it. She hated that she'd spent the week anticipating it.

She was coming to hate Saturdays. Allocated time for having sex.

She'd been married for four weeks and she'd had sex only three times.

It made her burn with humiliation to know that while he went through the motions with her, she came apart at his touch. But while she physically enjoyed every minute of their coming-together, emotionally she hated having to fight so hard to keep her passion contained and lie there passively beneath him. Hated that such passion had to be contained because he clearly felt none for her.

And she hated that she felt such excitement to be going out with him for a dinner date at Marcelo and Clara's quarters. She had a strong feeling this was at Clara's instigation and that the Englishwoman had refused to take no for an answer. It certainly wouldn't have come from Amadeo. He was still making an effort with her but the problem for Elsbeth now was that she could actually *see* what an effort it was. She didn't know what more she could do to win him over, and as she opened one of her cleverly fitted wardrobes disguised in her room's panelling, she rifled through the racks of beautiful clothes with his opinion in mind.

Oh, why had she decided to get herself ready? Usually she trusted the judgement of the beauty team she shared with her mother-in-law and sister-in-law, and wore whatever they picked out for her, but as this was a private meal and not an official engagement she'd given them all the evening off. After all, Alessia was in Madrid and Queen Isabella in Muscat so the team could actually go out and enjoy their Saturday evening.

The personal designer and seamstresses she also shared with her in-laws had collaborated on a swathe of beautiful dresses for her and the latest finished pieces had been added. A flash of vivid red caught her eye and when she pulled it off the rack her heart rose to her throat at how bold and daring, and *sexy,* the dress was.

Had the designer peered into her mind and seen the kind of dress Elsbeth so longed to wear?

Her heart sinking back down, she replaced it on the rack. This was a dress she would never wear. She couldn't. She was the future queen and it was imperative she dress with modesty at all times.

Sighing, she selected another, perfectly modest, dress with a side zip she could fasten herself.

She'd no sooner fastened the zip and checked her hair was in place when she heard the doorbell chime and her heart thumped into her ribs.

Amadeo was here.

CHAPTER FIVE

AMADEO ENTERED ELSBETH'S quarters and took a seat in her dayroom while he waited for her. It was the first time he'd been here since their evening at the Italian embassy and he was still unsure what had prompted him to suggest he come into her quarters rather than wait in their joint reception room as he usually did

His critical eye noticed a couple of changes to the room, the most obvious being an acrylic painting of a woman wearing a headdress of vivid flowers. It was good but, to his practised eye, naively painted and unoriginal. That it was displayed over the ornate five-hundred-year-old fireplace made him scratch his head as he was quite sure there had been a Renaissance painting there before.

His attention was drawn from the painting by movement and he turned his head to find Elsbeth entering the room, her motions so graceful she made no sound.

Wearing a high-necked, long-sleeved, form-fitting blue dress, so dark it could be mistaken for black, with what appeared to be silver stars patterned over it and falling to her feet, her hair was twisted back into her usual elegant chignon and her face subtly adorned with make-up. There was nothing special or unusual about her appearance. Nothing that could account for his throat catching and his intended polite greeting refusing to form.

'My apologies for making you wait,' she said in that soft, quiet voice he was slowly becoming accustomed to.

He cleared his throat and rose to his feet. 'You haven't. I was a few minutes early.' He'd been ready over an hour ago and had ended up watching the last half of an Italian football game to pass the time. He didn't even like football but he'd run out of distractions from the tingles that had plagued his body the entire day. What he wouldn't have given to be able to jump behind the wheel of a racing car and thrash it around Ceres National Racetrack and feel the machine bending to his will. Too dangerous, of course. He had done many laps of his country's racetrack, but those had been in ordinary cars in which he'd been obliged to resist the compulsion to put his foot flat on the accelerator and take them to their limits, and push himself to the limit too.

She stood before him. A waft of her perfume coiled into his senses. It was the same perfume she'd worn on their wedding day and every day

since. He must have become accustomed to it
for his dislike had vanished without him noticing. Probably familiarity, he supposed, even as
he resisted the temptation to dip his face into the
graceful curve of her neck and breathe it in more
deeply.

Yes. Familiarity. It could do that. He'd always
thought familiarity bred contempt or indifference
but was learning it could have the opposite effect
too. The opposite effect on him when it came to
his wife in any case.

It had to be all those working hours they spent
together causing it, he reasoned. No wonder his
senses were attuning themselves to her. She'd
arrived at his castle like a long-forgotten ghost,
bland and insignificant, barely seen or noticed,
but slowly her form was taking shape and solidi-
fying, and now he was always wholly aware of
her presence. And her absence. Slowly but surely,
she was coming to dominate his thoughts in the
weeknights and private days they spent apart. This
would have been as disconcerting as his awareness of her if he didn't have an answer for that
too, which was that Elsbeth was a conundrum
to be worked out. *That* was why she invaded his
thoughts. Amadeo had always insisted on knowing how things worked, from car engines to the
pendulum of a grandfather clock.

Elsbeth's insipidness was an act, he was certain of it, the smiley face a mask. Every day his

conviction grew that there was more between her ears than a little grey matter and a lot of hot air. Sometimes his fingers itched to rip the mask off her face and insist the real Elsbeth show herself.

'Where did you get that?' he asked, nodding at the painting above the fireplace.

'It was a gift from the Italian ambassador's daughter. Giuseppe told her how much I liked it so she sent it to me.'

'That's the danger of always having to be complimentary,' he observed. 'People take our compliments at face value. You didn't have to hang it—we have a room the size of the Blue Stateroom filled with gifts from the public where it can be stored. Your team should have told you that.' Noticing her gaze dart to the floor, he narrowed his eyes. '*Did* they tell you about the storeroom?'

A blush covering her cheeks, she nodded.

'Then why did you hang it?'

'Because I like it.' She chewed on her bottom lip before adding, 'But if you don't think it should be hung there I will have the old painting put back.'

'You *like* it?' He wouldn't have been more surprised if she'd actually pulled the vacuous smiley mask off her face with her nails.

She nodded again.

'Why?'

'I just do.'

'More than the original painting?'

Another nod.

His incredulity rocketing, he shook his head. 'Elsbeth, this is your home so what you hang on the walls is entirely up to you, but I'm curious why you would prefer the work of a fifteen-year-old schoolgirl over a Renaissance masterpiece.'

She raised her head and stared at the painting. 'I like the colour of the flowers.'

He recalled the waterlilies of the original painting. There had been something insipid about them he'd believed perfectly matched his wife.

'They're so bright and bold. And honest.' Was that a wistful note in her voice? 'And I like the expression in the woman's eyes. It's like she's saying, "Yes, I know, I'm wearing a headdress of flowers but aren't they wonderful?"' Her shoulders rose and she gave him a smile that contained no vacuity at all. 'Seeing it there makes me feel warm.'

Looking more closely at the painting, Amadeo began to see what she meant. There *was* something playful and knowing in the sitter's eyes.

And then he looked back into his wife's eyes and his throat caught again.

For an instant, her baby blue eyes were soft and warm, and in that instant he saw that behind them *was* a real woman of flesh and blood, with thoughts and opinions and dreams all of her own, and when the instant passed and the vacuous smile began to set itself back into place, his heart thumped and he snapped, *'Don't.'*

Elsbeth's smile froze on her lips.

What had she done to make him raise his voice at her like that?

Holding her breath, the individual beats of her heart pounded loudly in her ears while she watched Amadeo's shoulders and chest rise, and his head lift as he cast his gaze to the ceiling before his stare locked back on her.

'Only smile if you mean it.'

She stared at him, not knowing what he meant.

His eyes closed briefly again, the rise and fall of his shoulders and chest less pronounced. 'Elsbeth…' He grimaced and shook his head. 'I do not say this with the intention of hurting you, but all your smiles…they're too much. It seems to me that you hide behind them. They have their place when we're out on engagements, but when it's just you and me they're unnecessary. That painting makes you feel warm… Well, your smiles make me feel cold. Because they're not real. It's like being married to a blank canvas. I don't want a wife who hides behind a fake smile and agrees with everything I say. I want to know the real Elsbeth, the Elsbeth I just caught a glimpse of. I don't want to spend the rest of my life married to a stranger.'

The good Lord help her, she felt like a deer caught in the headlights. As hard as she tried to think, her thoughts were too many and too jumbled for any coherence. Panic swelling, she couldn't even think of something to say in response and, from the expression on his face, he was waiting for her to say something, but she didn't know what to say and, even if she could, she didn't know how to say it, not when she'd spent her whole life having it drilled into her that the best decorative adornment to a man's arm was a silent one.

After far too long of this excruciating silence he rubbed his knuckles to his forehead and sighed. 'We should go or we'll be late.'

Her cheeks automatically tried to pull her lips into a smile, but she stopped them by the skin of her teeth. 'I'm sorry.'

'And no more apologies,' he said roughly.

'Sorry,' she whispered. Like her smiles, apologies were an automatic response.

His grimace looked more rueful this time, the shake of his head less one of exasperation. 'Elsbeth...just be you. Okay?'

'What happens if you don't like the real me?' she surprised herself by saying.

She caught a glimmer of something like sympathy in his eyes. 'Then there will be no real change, will there?'

Surprisingly, the blunt honesty and directness of his answer didn't puncture her as deeply as it should.

Elsbeth liked Marcelo and Clara's quarters from the moment she stepped inside. As regal and chintzy as the rest of the castle, it had warm undertones she thought perfectly suited the couple who lived there, especially when Clara threw her arms around her.

Unprepared for such a gregarious welcome when the most she was used to was air kisses, she froze in Clara's tight embrace.

Laughing, Clara let her go, but only so far as to take Elsbeth's hand and drag her through to the bar at the far end of the dining room, speaking at a hundred miles an hour as she'd done during their walk together. As Elsbeth's English was minimal, she couldn't understand a word of it, but Clara's body language was enough for her to know how happy the Englishwoman was to host her, just as her body language on their walk had told her how happy she was in Elsbeth's company. It had been a lovely warming feeling and she'd been sorry when their walk had come to an end. When a glass of champagne was thrust into her hand and Clara held hers aloft with a beaming, 'Cheers,' she knew exactly what was meant and chinked her glass to it.

Somehow, with two native Italian speakers, an English speaker and herself a native French speaker, communication was no issue at all throughout the meal. Amadeo and Marcelo were both fluent in English and French and able to make any translations when Clara spoke too fast for Elsbeth to keep up or when Elsbeth's Eng-

lish failed her. By the time their main course was
cleared away she found she'd relaxed so much that
she was practically slouching in her chair!

But how could anyone fail to relax in such generous company? Generous in the sense that they
made her feel she'd completed their year simply
by being there. She'd never heard such laughter
before. Not real laughter. Clara had a ready smile
that Elsbeth studied, wondering how it differed to
her own smile that left Amadeo cold. And then
she saw for herself what the difference was—
Clara's smiles came naturally. There was nothing
practised in them, nor in her infectious laughter.

'You have had happy life?' she asked in tentative English. How else could it be possible for
someone to be so free within their own skin?

Clara pulled a face that made Elsbeth giggle.
She caught the sharp turn of Amadeo's face to
her from the corner of her eye but then Clara answered, saying, 'Gosh, no, before I met Marcelo
my life was hard. My mum died when I was a little girl, my father died when I wasn't much older
and left me in the care of my brother, who hated
me and packed me straight off to boarding school,
and then I got expelled from that horrible school,
which was excellent because I hated it there and,
quite frankly, it hated me, and then my brother
sold me to your cousin, King Pig and...'

Even with Amadeo translating as quickly as
Clara spoke, Elsbeth struggled to keep up, and

when it came to her cousin she could listen no more. 'I am very sorry for what he did to you.'

'It wasn't your fault,' Clara dismissed cheerfully. 'I'm just glad you weren't one of the women he sent to guard me and stop me escaping. I'd probably have to hate you then!'

Even Elsbeth laughed at that. 'I couldn't have,' she said when the laughter had died away. 'I would never have.'

'I know,' Clara said with a smile. 'And that's why I don't hate you. I imagine you suffered at his hands too?'

'I…' Elsbeth shrugged helplessly and strove for the correct English. 'All women suffer under Dominic.' It was the reason she'd been too cowardly to do anything to help Clara. The whole palace knew, despite Dominic's assertion that the Englishwoman he'd locked away was there willingly, that she was being held against her will and forced into marriage.

'Then I'm glad I only had to put up with him for a couple of weeks before Marcelo saved me.' She looked adoringly at her husband and was rewarded with a look so loving that Elsbeth felt a huge pang of envy and had to stop herself from glancing at Amadeo.

The sun would expire before he looked at her like that. Or consistently lean his body into hers the way Marcelo did with Clara. Or follow her every move with his eyes. This was a couple madly in love and lust, and it was almost painful to witness their constant need to touch each other. Were they afraid the other would disappear if they didn't have that anchoring contact?

She knew with instinctive clarity that the moment she and Amadeo left them they would be ripping each other's clothes off in the way she had seen couples behave in movies. Their lovemaking would be exuberant. Filthy. Loving. Everything her own couplings with Amadeo were not.

When this evening was over, Amadeo would come to her bed and they would do their duty and attempt to create the next heir to the Ceres throne. He would be naked but she would be wearing her nightdress. There would be no effort to remove it. She would climax. He would climax. And then he would wish her a goodnight and leave, and she would lie in her bed alone, her skin and pelvis still thrumming but her heart a gaping wound.

Lemon tarts were placed before them and, once demolished, coffee was brought out. Even two sugars and a thick swirling of cream couldn't disguise the underlying bitterness, but she sipped politely at it, unaware how sharp Clara's eyes really were until she said, for once at a speed Elsbeth could keep up with without translation, 'Don't drink it if you don't like it. What would you prefer?'

Amadeo twisted his stare back to his wife. Her cheeks had caught fire. The image of the coffee profiteroles at their wedding floated into his mind. 'You don't like coffee?'

She looked trapped, fearful blue gaze stark on his, white teeth slicing into her bottom lip. Instantly, he understood. To admit to disliking coffee—and, of course, she did dislike it or she wouldn't be looking so panicky—would be to admit to lying to him.

The usual irritation he felt when Elsbeth became all tongue-tied refused to form. He couldn't even summon irritation that she'd proven herself a liar, and about something as petty as coffee no less. Instead there was a weird compulsion to palm her scarlet cheeks and swear on his life that no harm would ever come to her.

Shaking the strange compulsion off, now aware that a tension had formed, that it wasn't only Elsbeth holding her breath but also his brother and sister-in-law, who likely had no idea why they were holding their breaths or any notion of where the tension had come from.

Placing his elbow on the table, he propped his chin on his hand and murmured in French, 'You know, Elsbeth, confession is good for the soul?'

Her stare remained stark on him.

'Is there something you wish to confess?' he continued. 'Something, say, about marrying into a family of coffee fiends, in a country of coffee connoisseurs, and feeling obliged to hide your aversion to the glorious black stuff so as not to be drowned in a vat of it? Because, let me assure you, we haven't drowned non-coffee-drinkers here for at least two hundred years.'

A few beats later, having had to wait for the punchline while Marcelo translated for her, Clara gave a bark of laughter. The sound of it seemed to snap Elsbeth out of her panic. In an instant, her features were transformed. Her lips curved into a smile that tugged at her eyes, her whole face lighting up into something so beautiful that Amadeo's heart skipped a beat. A giggle flew out of her mouth, sounding like music to his ears—he *hadn't* imagined her earlier one—and then her hand flew to cover it.

Her shoulders shook a few times before she removed her hand and looked him squarely in the eye. 'Okay. I confess. I hate coffee.'

'And coffee profiteroles?'

Her cheeks caught fire again but she nodded. 'Coffee in all its forms.'

It was on the tip of his tongue to tell her she should have spoken up before, that approving items she disliked on her own wedding menu was masochistic, but he held it back. She would take it as criticism and slip back into her vacuous shell.

How he could be so certain of this, he didn't know, and nor did he know what it was about criticism that affected her so much, but he did know this was not something he could draw out of her with an audience.

In his mind flashed an unbidden image of stripping Elsbeth of all the shields and masks she hid behind. It was an image that sent a short but potent stab of lust burning through him.

CHAPTER SIX

AMADEO SHIFTED HIS weight off Elsbeth and rolled onto his back. It was a struggle to catch his breath.

Doing his duty was incrementally feeling less like duty. Less like a chore.

As she always did after they'd come together, Elsbeth lay silently beside him. He knew she'd climaxed, was becoming attuned to the signs, the shortening breaths, the barely perceptible mewing, was learning the motions that tipped her over the edge and made her thicken around him and her fingers press into his back. Afterwards, she would lay her hands neatly by her sides, the only sign that she'd enjoyed what they'd just shared the rapid beats of her heart pounding through their joined chests until he rolled off her and she folded her hands neatly over her abdomen and lay in silence until he wished her a goodnight.

Her hands were neatly folded over her abdomen now.

What was she thinking? Her mind wasn't the blank canvas he'd believed. The wind-up doll persona was only a persona. So what was she thinking as she lay silently beside him, waiting for him to leave? Was she imagining how she would spend the next day? Thinking of her family? Formulating maths equations that had the potential to change the world?

Or was she thinking of him, as he was thinking of her? Was she silently encouraging him to go and leave her in peace so she could sleep? Was she wondering why he hadn't left already? She wouldn't ask him to leave. His wife might be an enigma to him but he knew that much.

'How did you suffer under Dominic?' he asked. The question had swirled in his mind since their earlier conversation at dinner.

She took a long time to answer. 'I didn't say I'd suffered. I said women suffer under him. I spoke out of turn.'

'So you didn't suffer under him?'

'It depends on your definition of suffering.'

'Why are you prevaricating?'

She fell silent again.

Trying to keep the frustration from his voice, he said, 'Elsbeth, I am trying to understand you. I *want* to understand you. But you don't make it easy. Stories have circulated about the House of Fernandez for a long time.'

'What kind of stories?'

'That Dominic rules with an iron fist—not his people but those within his sphere: his fam-

ily and the courtiers and staff who work for him.
That his sister Catalina fled Monte Cleure and re-
fuses to return while he is alive because he used
to beat her. That he's paid off a number of lovers
to gag them from sharing tales of his depravity.
I've known the man all my life and none of the
stories about him come as a surprise. His reputation alone was enough for me and my parents to
refuse talks of him marrying my sister, and that
was before he kidnapped Clara.'

'You refused permission for Alessia to marry
him?'

'I wouldn't marry my worst enemy to him.
Clara calls him King Pig which is, I think, far
too generous a title. He would have forced her
to marry him and forced himself on her if Marcelo hadn't rescued her. And now I have told you
what I think, I would like to hear your thoughts
about him.'

She shifted slightly, half turning her body towards him. 'Why do you want my thoughts?'

'Why would I not?' He took a deep breath to
quell his frustration.

'I am coming to see that things are different
here.'

'What do you mean?'

'The way you treat your women. Here, they are
allowed opinions, yes?'

'So are women in Monte Cleure,' he countered.
'There is complete equality, written in law.'

Through the darkness, he could feel her gaze searching his. 'Not quite.'

'There are no barriers to your women doing whatever they want.'

'Not ordinary women, no,' she agreed softly. 'But royal women aren't ordinary women. Dominic loosened many of the old laws when he took the throne and fully emancipated the women of Monte Cleure so that all discrimination was outlawed, and he was feted by the European press and governments for it, but he tightened the laws regarding the royal family itself. Any member of the royal family closer than a third cousin is not allowed to marry, leave the country or hold a bank account without his written permission. Fathers and husbands of the Fernandez family have effectively been granted ownership of their wives and daughters but Dominic has absolute power over us all, so you must forgive me when I say that the opinions I have of him can never be spoken. If he heard about them he would kill me.'

It was the longest speech she'd ever made to him and, as she'd spoken, an intelligent, eloquent woman had emerged, so intelligent and eloquent that the words themselves took a few moments to penetrate.

'Are you being serious?' He'd known Dominic was a tyrant but what Elsbeth described was medieval, there was no other word for it, a system of governance and power that hadn't existed in his own country in that form for centuries.

Her eyes rang. 'If he can kidnap a British citizen, what do you think he would do to one of his own subjects?'

'But you're no longer one of his subjects. You're a Ceresian Princess now, and future Queen Consort.'

'For now,' she said wistfully.

'For always. You're my wife.' For the first time, acknowledging Elsbeth as his wife didn't make him shudder internally. Was it acceptance evoking this softening towards her?

'Amadeo, I am not a fool. You don't like me. If I don't give you children then in a year, two years, three years at most, you will see that things have settled between your country and Monte Cleure, and that sending me back home will not result in the trade and diplomatic war you married me to avoid. You will have done your bit for your country and there will be no good reason for you to keep me.'

Astounded, Amadeo sat up and turned the bedside light on so he could look at her properly.

Elsbeth clasped the bedsheet covering her and tried to breathe naturally through the thudding of her heart. Speaking her thoughts out loud was a new thing for her. She could never have uttered such things at home, and while she knew there would be no punishment from Amadeo, she didn't know what kind of reaction she was about to receive for speaking her mind.

Closing his eyes, he breathed deep and hard, his smooth olive chest rising, the defined pectoral muscles tightening. Quickly, she averted her gaze from his body, not wanting to be caught staring at him improperly. Safer not to look for her own sake too. It did strange things to her, made her feel liquid inside, much the same way his touch did. Made the wound in her heart throb with something that felt very much like a pang of yearning, and there was already too much yearning at this moment in her.

Amadeo would normally have left her bed by now. Nothing inside her felt right when he was naked beside her. Before the event, her body would thrill with anticipation. Afterwards, a cold desolation would form in her chest when he moved off her that ran counter to the tingles from her climax which would last for hours. Pleasure and pain in one Amadeo-sized dose. At least alone she could hold his pillow to her chest and curl into it, a sorry substitute for the warm hunk of man she craved to cuddle into in those hours after sex but better than nothing. Better than feeling the tingles and desolation with him still lying beside her without a single part of his body touching hers. One minute as intimate as a man and a woman could be, the next, the connection severed.

The longer their marriage went on, the more

grateful she was that she slept alone. She didn't know how she'd endure sleeping night after night beside a man who only touched her to make a baby. Better the way things were: get the job done then sleep apart. No false promises. No false affection. Less time for her heart and body to crave more. Less chance of further hurt.

She wished he would leave so she could cuddle into his pillow and self-soothe.

Instead, his clear green gaze locked back on hers. 'I don't know how things are done in the House of Fernandez, but in my family we take our wedding vows seriously. Till death us do part. That's what we both promised.'

She took a long breath before summoning the courage to voice her deepest fear. 'What if I don't conceive?'

'You are twenty-four. I'm thirty-two,' he said dismissively. 'We are both fit and healthy. There is nothing to suggest we will have trouble conceiving.'

'But what if we do?'

'Then we cross that bridge when we come to it.'

'You might choose a path that doesn't include me when we've crossed it. There is no affection or shared history to bind you to me.'

His eyes penetrating, he shook his head. 'But that works both ways.'

'How?'

'If you choose to end our marriage there will be nothing I can do about it.'

The idea was so preposterous that she gave a short laugh. 'And where would I go? What would I do? I own nothing but my name.' Elsbeth had a team of domestic staff who catered to her every whim, a team of clerical staff to manage every minute of her working life, a personal designer and seamstresses to create bespoke clothing for her, an unlimited credit card for everything else, but she didn't have a cent in her own name. Not one cent. The credit card could be turned off in an instant.

'That would be up to you.' He climbed off the bed and reached for his robe. 'This is Ceres, not Monte Cleure. I have committed my life to you as your husband, not your ruler. We have obligations to each other and the monarchy, rules we must both abide by, but no rights over the other. I hope you will abide by those obligations but I cannot force you to do so. You are your own autonomous woman.'

Was it wishful thinking on her part that he sounded sincere?

Or was it the dim light turning Amadeo's chiselled features into plains and shadows that made the gape in her heart yearn even harder for something she could never have?

Something she must train her heart into believing she no longer wanted.

A week later, dressed in an old pair of black shorts, Amadeo carried his coffee out onto his bedroom's balcony. The early morning sun was rising in the warming sky, the castle sleeping. He'd woken to duskiness with a strange fluttering in his stomach. Unable to fall back asleep and unwilling to break this rare moment of solitude by calling in his staff, he'd made his own coffee… okay, *made* was a loose term seeing as a pot with fresh beans was prepared for him each night so only a button needed to be pressed to get it working, but the intention was there.

The balcony overlooked his sprawling private garden. Standing at the stone balustrade, he gazed out at the immaculate lawn surrounded by orderly hedges and symmetrically arranged flower beds, and waited for this momentary peace to settle the fluttering.

When a figure appeared on the lawn his heart thumped as he blinked to clear the mirage. But the figure remained and the flutters became heavier. Denser.

It was Elsbeth.

Amadeo's quarters being set over hers, the garden was the one space they shared. He'd debated before their wedding whether or not to partition it but dismissed it as unnecessary as he so rarely used it.

Cradling a mug between her hands, she stepped barefoot over thick grass damp with early morning dew, her dishevelled blonde hair hanging down to her shoulders. Unlike the variant of modest vir-

ginal white nightdress she always wore when he
joined her in bed, that morning she was wearing a pair of short, red and white checked pyjamas, the bottoms loosely wrapped around supple
golden thighs.

His own bare feet had descended the iron stairs
from his balcony before he could stop them.

She must have sensed him for she whipped
around, and any chance of turning back was gone.
Even with the distance between them he could see
the colour rise up her cheeks.

As he strode lazily towards her, the beats of
his heart accelerating with every step, he soaked
in every inch of the body usually hidden beneath
modest clothing, the swell of unhindered breasts
pushing against the simple cotton of the pyjama
T-shirt in a way he'd never noticed beneath her
virgin nightdresses.

The urge to greet her with a kiss was strong
enough to make him grind to a halt two paces
before her.

They never kissed outside of the bed, not even
the polite air-kisses of acquaintances. By unspo-
ken agreement, physical contact between them
was strictly limited to their Saturday night sex
window, and that in itself was limited too. Did
Elsbeth ever wish for more…?

He breathed in deeply through his nose and
summoned a half-smile. 'You're up early.'

She returned the smile shyly. 'I'm an early riser.'

He'd be an early riser too, in more ways than one, if he woke up next to this ravishing, tousle-haired, sexy creature...

Sexy? Elsbeth?

Staring into those baby blue eyes with a tightening chest and thickening loins, it came to him with something akin to shock that the stirrings of arousal he suffered with increasing frequency around her were proof that, on some level, he already found her sexy.

In her own unique, quiet way, Elsbeth was truly ravishing and, as all these thoughts built in his head, the eyes he found himself unable to break the lock of his gaze from darkened and Elsbeth's slender throat extended, and suddenly he knew, in that long, charged beat of silence, that his steadily growing attraction was reciprocated...right until she blinked her stare away from him and drank from her mug.

When she met his stare again a moment later, whatever he'd seen in the baby blue eyes had gone.

Amadeo searched hard but no, it had vanished with no trace of it ever having existed.

He swore loudly in his head. He was getting the hots for his wife, and she was standing there sipping her drink with her usual calm demeanour, waiting for him to speak—she still only rarely instigated conversations—and with no hint whatsoever of what was going on in her head.

Elsbeth was fast becoming the most infuriating, intriguing, exasperating woman he'd ever known. When he'd been busy being irritated by her fake smiles he'd failed to notice the sheer stillness with which she held herself. Having always prided himself on his self-control, he had to accept that Elsbeth was a master of composure who made him look and, more importantly, feel like an amateur.

Determined to take back control of himself, he nodded at the mug in her hand and idly said, 'Coffee?'

Sheepish mischief flashed in her eyes. 'Tea.'

Mio Dio, that hint of mischief was as unexpected as if she'd suddenly started doing cartwheels across the lawn and, damn it, as sexy as hell.

'I thought only the Brits drank tea?' he teased, refusing to allow this fresh hit of arousal derail his determination for control.

She gave a delicate one-shouldered shrug. 'I always wanted to be British.'

'Really? Why?'

'I love their gardens.'

That amused him. 'Really? You wanted to be British because of their gardens?' He'd never met a woman under the age of thirty who had any interest in gardens whatsoever.

'The British love their gardens and make such

an effort with their flower beds, and their seasons are so much more pronounced than in Monte Cleure so you can watch them unfold like a living calendar. They have the barren wasteland of winter, but then the first appearance of shoots appear in early spring and then, by the time summer comes, their gardens just bloom with colour. Even their autumns are beautiful, when the leaves change and everywhere's all russet and gold.'

Although delivered as quietly as she always spoke, there was an animation in her voice and a light in her eyes he'd never heard or seen before.

'What do you think of my—our—garden?' Seeing her eyes widen fractionally before her lips started pulling into the fake smile that had rarely made an appearance all that week, he stopped it fully forming by shaking his head and giving a short laugh. 'Don't try and lie. You don't like it. I can tell.'

Her mouth dropped open. 'How?'

Now he was the one to shrug. 'It is something I have noticed. When you're afraid you're going to say something you believe could be incriminating, you put your mask on so you can hide your real thoughts behind it.' Strangely, the mask she used to hide behind was the only time he was able to read her. Stripped of it, her composure was too strong for him to read anything she didn't want to give away. 'It's okay,' he added nonchalantly. 'I understand it will take time before you trust that you can speak freely with me.'

Their talk the last time they'd shared her bed had opened Amadeo's eyes to the factors that had made his wife the way she was. He assumed it was the knowledge of those factors that had seen him spend a full week of engagements with her without once getting irritated by her in those few times her mask had slipped back on. A telephone conversation with Dominic's estranged sister, the Princess Catalina, had revealed Elsbeth had spoken the truth about the power Dominic had extended to himself over his family. Things were worse there than even he'd suspected.

Dominic was playing a clever game, he grudgingly admitted: principality-wide reform to keep the investment flowing in—Monte Cleure was a billionaires' playground—but behind the scenes turning the House of Fernandez back into a medieval court where he reigned supreme. Centuries ago, Amadeo's ancestors had had the same uncontested power over their people…until the people had risen and toppled them. He doubted such a toppling would happen to Dominic, not while his people enjoyed the highest incomes and lowest taxes in the western world. Only an internal coup would oust him.

Elsbeth's father was Dominic's uncle, the most senior royal courtier in the House of Fernandez. Any coup would need his backing, but when he'd said this to Catalina she'd laughed. 'Your father-in-law is Dominic's biggest supporter. It will never happen.'

The uncle of a tyrannical monster would be grandfather to any children Amadeo and Elsbeth had. It was a thought that sickened him and he was trying hard not to let his reaction further colour his feelings for the man's daughter. Although his growing attraction to her was undeniable, attraction was a chemical thing that sooner or later would burn itself out. His marriage, however, would last until death. Amadeo would never forget that Elsbeth was a Fernandez by blood, contaminated to her soul, but he had to believe he could come to accept her as a Berruti. As his wife.

Trying to loosen the sudden tightness in his chest with a long inhale, he gave a quick encouraging smile. 'Go on, tell me. What would you change about our garden?'

Her face screwed up a fraction before she blurted out, 'All of it.'

'It's that bad?'

'It's not bad at all. It's very ordered and pretty.'

'But you say it as if ordered and pretty were a bad thing,' he countered, catching her out with the tone of her own words.

'They're not if you like that kind of thing,' she protested, half laughing. 'It's just that I like the English country cottage style where there's much less order and different varieties, sizes and colours of flowers are clustered together all higgledy-piggledy.'

He couldn't help but smile at her turn of phrase. Higgledy-piggledy. He would never have imagined his neat, ultra-composed wife would consider higgledy-piggledy to be a good thing. 'Have you spent much time in England?'

She shook her head ruefully. 'None at all. But I watch all their gardening shows. You went to boarding school there, didn't you?'

He nodded.

'And are their gardens as beautiful as in the television shows?'

'I didn't take any notice of them.'

'Why not?'

'Because I was a teenage boy and flowers and gardens were not my thing,' he answered drily.

He caught a sudden knowing flash in her eyes. 'No, I don't suppose they were,' she said, and in that instant Amadeo was taken back to his adolescent boarding school years, where he'd experienced a degree of freedom away from his country and castle walls that had never been repeated. Images flashed in his mind of lazy weekends spent in the local town with friends, catching the eye of pretty girls with knowing smiles, gropes and fumbles by riverbanks, illicit cigarettes and smuggled alcohol.

Those had been halcyon days of rampant hormones, the constant prickles of awareness capable of turning into full arousal at the sight of a short skirt rolled up a few extra inches, and as Amadeo gazed into his wife's eyes he realised there was something similar in the thrill of awareness that so often zipped through him for her as he'd felt in his teenage years. It had to be the thrill of forbidden fruit, because was anything more thrilling than when it was forbidden? Would he still desire to speed full throttle around the Ceres National Racetrack if it wasn't against the rules and so forbidden?

And would he still desire Elsbeth as much as he was growing to if he hadn't made her forbidden to himself?

Amadeo was so locked in his memories and thoughts that he only realised silence had elapsed between them again when Elsbeth smoothed her hair and delicately cleared her throat. 'I should take a shower and get some breakfast,' she murmured.

He snapped himself back to the present.

Walking in step, they reached the bottom of his stairs, beneath which lay the short path to Elsbeth's French doors.

Their eyes met at the point where they went their separate ways.

'Well…' she said with another of those graceful shrugs. 'I will see you later.'

He gazed again at the elegant swan of her neck.

His mouth watered to imagine tracing his tongue over it.

Amadeo was halfway up the iron steps when he looked down to where Elsbeth was about to step into her quarters. 'Elsbeth,' he called.

She looked up at him.

It was on the tip of his tongue to invite her to join him for breakfast. 'Enjoy your day.'

A soft smile played on her lips. 'And you.'

And then she vanished from his sight.

CHAPTER SEVEN

ELSBETH'S LEGS WERE still shaking when she stepped out of the shower and wrapped a large fluffy towel around herself. They'd started shaking the moment she'd closed her French doors and finally escaped her half-naked, rampantly masculine husband.

Since their wedding, she'd taken an early morning walk around her garden every day and not once had she been disturbed by anyone. The garden was the only place in the castle where she could be alone without feeling lonely. As the weeks had passed, she'd redesigned it in her mind, imagining it as a riot of colour with quirky statues and hammocks, occasionally allowing herself to dare to dream about the children who might one day play in it. She'd become so used to being alone with only her thoughts and early morning birdsong that when she'd sensed another human presence and spun around to find Amadeo walking down the iron steps, she'd been completely unable to control the contraction in her body that had felt much too much like joy to be healthy.

She'd barely held it together from that point.

When he'd strode over the lawn to her, she'd inwardly cringed at being caught wearing pyjamas more suited to a teenage girl than a princess, had been unable to stop her mother's stern voice repeating in her ear the warning given *ad nauseam* in the weeks before the wedding. 'A prince expects his wife to be a princess at all times.'

He hadn't looked disapprovingly at her though. In fact...

If she didn't know better, she'd think the hooded glimmer in his eyes had been desire. She must have imagined it. How could he desire her when being civil was an effort for him?

For the first time though, she hadn't sensed the effort. It had been a strangely intimate encounter, filled with a weird, indefinable tension that had only added weight to the heavy wings of the butterflies loose in her belly. It hadn't helped that Amadeo had been practically naked, only a pair of low-slung black shorts covering him. It had taken every fibre of her being to stop herself openly staring at him, hardly daring to allow her eyes to skim over the deeply tanned broad, hard chest and flat brown nipples, or the washboard abdomen where dark hair gathered beneath his navel and thickened as it lowered to the waistband of his shorts. Lord, just to think of him like that was enough to send heat flushing her skin again, and she sank onto the bathroom chair and gripped her hair.

She needed to banish the butterflies and train her body better. She was married to a man who disliked her, despised her family and had admitted he'd never wanted to marry her. To have all these feelings for a man like that was dangerous. Especially when he was her husband.

'Out!'

Amadeo glared at his sister-in-law, who was sitting in the umpire's chair casting judgement on his serve. 'It was not.'

'Yes, it was. Second serve.'

Taking his place back on the line, he lobbed the tennis ball into the air and thwacked it.

'Out. Game to Marcelo.'

'You don't know how to umpire,' Amadeo seethed.

'And you don't know how to serve,' she retorted chirpily.

He resisted the furious urge to hurl his racket at the clay court by the skin of his teeth and readied himself for his brother's serve.

In less than an hour Marcelo had thrashed him three sets to nil, the worst defeat Amadeo had ever suffered.

He blamed Elsbeth. Or tried to. Damn it, she was getting under his skin. He'd spent the morning with the concentration span of a goldfish, official paperwork shoved to one side unread, the image of her, all sexy and dishevelled in those sexy little pyjamas a memory he could not rid himself of. The knowledge that she was doing whatever she was doing in the quarters below his had only added to the infuriating distraction.

Reasonably telling himself that exercise would help his mindset, he'd bribed his brother out of his marital bed for a game of tennis, but instead of the usual outcome where a five match set between them would go down to the wire...

Damn it! He couldn't even blame it on Clara's blatantly biased umpiring. He'd been useless.

Amadeo hated losing, but not as much as he hated losing when it was his own damn fault.

Elsbeth's jitters were regaining strength. The clock was ticking to Duty Night hour. Amadeo would be here in three hours.

She hadn't stopped thinking about him all day, and it was much worse than his usual crowding of her head. A long walk in the castle's woods hadn't helped and nor had a swim in the family's private indoor pool. Thank the Lord they had a week free from engagements coming up. No being stuck in a car with him for hours each day and glued to his side for hours more.

Fed up with pacing her quarters and resisting the urge to go back outside and loiter in the garden—she didn't want to look as if she was hoping for his company—she decided to take another shower before her dinner was brought to her from the castle kitchen, but that didn't help either. Lathering her naked body only brought home how badly her skin craved Amadeo's touch.

Oh, this was madness!

Stomping to her wardrobe, she yanked a green maxi dress off the rack—no point putting on a virgin nightdress this early—and had just slipped it over her head when there was a tap on her bedroom door.

'Come in,' she called.

One of her domestic staff entered. 'His Highness is here.'

Her heart slammed against her ribs. 'Amadeo?'

'Yes.'

'What does he want?'

The maid gave her a look that clearly said it was not her job to question him.

Panic clutched her like a vice and she immediately began to pace.

He was two and a half hours early! She wasn't ready! How could she receive him like this, with her hair all wet and not even any moisturiser on her face? *Look* at her face! It was all red from the heat of the shower!

It was catching sight of the sweet maid waiting patiently at the door that calmed her.

She couldn't help that she wasn't ready for him,

and she could at least take consolation that her dress was perfectly modest, if a little more colourful than the clothing she endured on their engagements.

With the butterflies all loose again in her belly and her heart beating like a hummingbird's wings, she found Amadeo in the dayroom looking at the latest picture she'd had hung there.

Her hummingbird heart rose up her throat. She didn't know if she would ever get used to the thrill that shivered through her whenever she set eyes on him, her internal reaction the same whatever his state of dress. That evening, he was wearing his usual attire of shirt, this one a pale blue, and trousers, but had abandoned the tie and jacket he would usually match with it. His thick black hair was tousled and swept to the side, and…

Oh, was it any wonder she couldn't control her pulse around him? Just *look* at the man. She defied any woman not to get all hot and flustered around him.

For the first time in her life, Elsbeth was grateful for her upbringing. At least she'd long ago had to master the art of self-control, and she channelled everything her mother and the other senior ladies of the House of Fernandez had taught her to contain the turbulence and keep it hidden from her face and outer body.

He turned his head, a lazy half-smile forming. 'Nice painting.'

'You like it?' It occurred to her that she'd not had the slightest concern whether he would or would not.

It wasn't just words from him, she realised with a jolt. Amadeo *didn't* try to control her.

'I'm sure I'll like it once you've explained why *you* like it. You can explain while we eat.'

Eat? *We*? Was he saying…?

'I thought I would join you for dinner. Unless you have other plans?' he added with a knowing smile and a raised brow.

Her hummingbird heart expanded and rose so quickly that she almost threw it up.

Elsbeth took a moment to compose herself before attempting to mimic his nonchalance, but as her only plans had been to eat her dinner then probably have another shower to calm her nerves and get herself ready for his appearance in her bedroom, the only word that came out of her mouth was, 'Okay.'

Amadeo nearly laughed out loud, but not with humour. *Okay?* Was that it?

While finally admitting to himself that his wife was sexy had flicked a switch in his brain that had meant Elsbeth was all he could think about, she'd continued with her day, blithe and oblivious. After his disastrous tennis match, he'd sat on his balcony with a cold beer in a futile attempt to calm the explosive feelings shooting through him. Only when an hour had passed did he realise he hadn't wrenched his eyes from the garden and that the reason his stomach lurched at every sound and movement was because he was waiting for her to appear.

And that had been the moment he'd said, *To hell with it*. This thing he had for his wife clearly wasn't going to disappear just because he commanded it. It was time to do something about it. And so he'd strode back inside, giving orders to his butler, and hit the shower. He could share a meal with his wife before sex. That wasn't breaking any rule.

'Is this a new dinner set?' he asked once their first course had been served. It was nothing like the fine china the family ate from, a variant of which had been given to Elsbeth for her personal use. He wondered if she'd ransacked the storeroom.

'It's from the art college we went to a couple of weeks ago.'

His brows drew together. At one of their engagements they had awarded prizes to graduating students at Ceres' top art school. 'This won an award?'

'No, but it was on display.'

'I don't remember seeing it.' As far as he remembered, it had been the usual paintings and ceramics exhibited. He had no recollection of crockery displayed that had comedic cactuses painted on them.

'It's all still a novelty for me,' she said kindly. 'I imagine you've been undertaking engagements for so many years it's become monotonous.'

'Undoubtedly,' he agreed. Their coming engagement-free week would be a welcome break from the monotony. The summer months, August in particular, were always exceptionally busy with engagements, the Ceresian tourist sites organising events to entice visitors, businesses and the charities the Berrutis patroned opening their doors and gardens to the public. Amadeo, his siblings and their parents, highly aware their positions were dependent on the Ceresian public's goodwill, tried to attend as many of the different events as time would allow. Now that September had arrived, the children had returned to school and tourist numbers reduced, the number of engagements would significantly reduce, allowing them to concentrate more on their specific charities and the non-public-facing part of royal life.

He looked closely at his side plate before looking back at Elsbeth, a burn in his loins as he imagined stripping her naked and examining her with the same close scrutiny. *Dio*, that sleeveless dress she was wearing... Like all the other clothes she wore, it showed not the slightest hint of breast or cleavage, only her arms and shoulders exposed, but what little flesh was on display was enough to make his fingers itch to dip into the shallow where her graceful neck met her collarbone.

Swallowing the moisture that had filled his throat, the knowledge they would soon retreat to her bedroom a pulse that throbbed in every part of him, he forced his attention to stay on the conversation in hand. 'Did the student offer it to you?'

'No, I got in touch and asked if it was for sale.' At his raised brow of surprise, Elsbeth felt a pang of anxiety. 'Is that not the done thing? No one said I shouldn't.' She meant Lia, her private secretary, who reported to Amadeo's private secretary. Lia hadn't batted an eyelid when Elsbeth asked about the possibility of buying the set. Lia had sorted it all out for her, including arranging for the talented student to dine with Elsbeth two nights ago so Elsbeth could get an insight into her quirky, creative mind. She didn't want to get Lia into trouble for any of this.

He gave a bemused shake of his head before reaching for his red wine. 'You are not answerable to me. How you spend your money and furnish your quarters and instruct your staff is up to you.'

She blew out the breath she'd been holding. This was the first purchase she'd ever made for herself with her own taste in mind. She'd taken a leap of faith that Amadeo had meant it when he told her she was an autonomous woman.

She had to admit that buying the dinner set had felt amazing. She'd actually *felt* autonomous. Inviting the student to dine with her had been a new experience too. In the palace, she'd shared her parents' quarters, every minute of her day controlled and decided for her.

What felt even more amazing though, were the thrills racing through her to have Amadeo's full, sole attention. Dangerous though. She knew that. Her head, at least, was clear, and knew not to read anything into the looks from him that made her bones melt. She was projecting her own desire for him onto him. To imagine anything more was to set herself up for a fall. That he was here, spending time with her outside work duties… She mustn't read anything into it. He'd probably been bored.

He speared a tiny tomato. 'The things you have added and replaced to your quarters—the ones I've seen—are all striking and modern. You seem to have…eclectic taste,' he added drily before casting his gaze around the pastel pink dining room. 'Tell me honestly, what do you think of your quarters' furnishings and decorations?'

'Do I have to?'

He grinned. 'You should blame Alessia. I put her in charge. I thought that, as a young woman, she'd have a better idea of what you'd like than I would. Maybe it would have been better to put Clara in charge.'

A tiny giggle escaped from her mouth before she even knew it was coming. 'I would have liked to see the results of that.'

'I wouldn't.'

That did make her laugh, and as her eyes met

Amadeo's clear green gaze, a rumble of laughter spilled from his lips and hit her veins like a pulse of energy.

How could she possibly *feel* laughter? It didn't make any sense but it felt as real as if it were a living entity. Everything about him did, from his voice to his slow smiles to the glimmer in his eyes. She didn't just see them, she felt them through the buzz in her veins and the pulses of heat that came close to sucker-punching her.

She'd never imagined a person could be so in tune with another and so alive in their company, but she knew she wouldn't betray herself so long as she concentrated on their conversation. What she mustn't do was think about what would happen once their meal finished, but then telling herself not to do that immediately made her think of it and, as she gazed into his eyes, heat coiled its way from deep in her pelvis and into her veins as a sudden image flashed through her mind of Amadeo following her down the corridor, closing the bedroom door and taking her into his arms…

'Are you okay?'

Her heart thumped and she blinked sharply to pull her brain back into focus but that pulled Amadeo's dreamily handsome face back into focus too and sent her pulses soaring all over again. Grabbing her glass of wine, she smiled brightly. 'Of course.'

'You're sure?' His probing stare bored into her. 'You look flushed.'

'It's a little warm in here, that's all.' She drained her wine in one swallow.

She was lying. Amadeo knew it. The vacuous smile was the giveaway. And the faint tremor in her hand as she put her empty glass on the table and reached for the bottle to top it up. Another improvement, he noted. A month ago, she would have gone thirsty.

He knew she was lying but didn't care, because at the same moment her cheeks had turned the same colour as the tomatoes his lobster had been served with, her wide eyes had held his, darkening and pulsing with the same heat that had plagued him since he'd spotted her from his balcony that morning.

His euphoria lasted seconds, the time it took for her to have a sip of her replenished wine and fix her eyes back on him.

The only thing to read in them was friendliness.

Damn it, whatever he'd seen had gone *again*.

He watched her even more closely over their next course, looking for even a flicker of the desire he now thought he'd seen twice that day. But there was nothing. She answered his questions about what she liked so much about the latest painting she'd hung on the wall with the same animation as when she'd explained her love for the ambassador daughter's painting, but there was no intimacy in her body language. She didn't subconsciously lean forward to be closer to him or play with her hair. When he deliberately rested his hand at the mid-point between them on the table, she didn't inch her fingers closer to it. Her eyes didn't linger on him with anything approaching seduction.

This was driving him crazy! He could be sharing a meal with his sister for all the attraction Elsbeth was displaying towards him.

Had those glimmers of desire been conjured by his overinflated ego being unable to accept that a woman could share his bed and keep her feelings compartmentalised? He could laugh at the irony that his intention at the outset of his marriage to a Fernandez was for the whole thing to be kept compartmentalised. It bruised his ego that Elsbeth was perfectly content with the separation he'd imposed while he was the one suffering.

Draining his wine, he determined that his suffering wouldn't last for long. Whatever else she might feel, he knew Elsbeth had a basic desire for him. It had been there, just like his own initial basic desire, from the night they'd consummated their marriage. That was simple chemistry. Put two willing, sexually compatible people in a bed together and their bodies would do what needed to be done. All he needed to do was draw that basic desire out of her into the flame currently consuming him, because doing what needed to be done wasn't enough any more. He wanted more. Much more. He just needed to gorge himself on her and then he would be satisfied and this strange fever for her would cool back to its original apathy.

CHAPTER EIGHT

THIS WAS HORRENDOUS.

Elsbeth had never in her entire life worked so hard at maintaining outward composure. It wasn't just dining alone with Amadeo causing it, it was all the signals her needy brain was interpreting. His stare didn't leave her face, his green eyes seemed to drink her in with an appreciation she *must* be imagining.

When he put his first mouthful of their divine dessert into his mouth and slowly sucked the dark chocolate off his spoon, the motion was so sensual she came close to spontaneously combusting.

How on earth was she supposed to keep control over herself when he joined her in bed for their Duty later, when just watching him eat was turning her on so much that she could feel arousal over every inch of her skin?

Stop looking at me!

Quickly eating her chocolate torte in the hope he'd follow her lead as if by osmosis, she was ready to scream when she noticed he still had over half his portion left.

Was he doing it deliberately?

She pushed her empty bowl to one side and determined to distract herself from the eroticism of watching Amadeo eat. 'Now you know I like bold and quirky art and furnishings and English gardens, it is only fair you tell me of the things you like. I assume motor racing is one. I mean as a sport and not just as an investment.'

He pulled the spoon out of his mouth. 'You assume correctly.'

'Cars or bikes?'

'Both, but cars are my preference. I've attended nearly every Grand Prix held on Ceres National Racetrack since I was a small child. One of my earliest memories is watching a race with my father and being jealous that he was allowed to present the trophy and champagne to the winner on the podium while I was forced to stay in my seat.'

'I bet it was a good seat.'

The spoon sliced back through the torte that still wasn't disappearing quickly enough for Elsbeth's sanity. 'The best in the stadium. We were so close to the track I was made to wear ear defenders.'

The divine lips closed over the chocolate-filled spoon. All she could do was cross her legs tightly and take another drink of her wine and hope it cooled her down. 'Have you ever driven a racing car?' she asked.

Remembering the school project in which he'd taken the lead in building a go-cart and then made the mistake of telling his parents and being instantly forbidden from driving it, Amadeo shook his head. 'It's considered too dangerous an activity for the heir to the Ceres throne.'

The point had been drilled into him that being heir meant he must not do anything that could endanger him. He'd had to watch from the stands while the go-cart he'd designed and engineered in his sixth form years was driven over the finish line in second place by his second-in-command. If he'd been driving it, he would have won. That wasn't arrogance talking—and Amadeo would be the first to admit he had as much arrogance as testosterone in him—just cold fact. Before he'd been banned, he'd test-driven it around the track. His lap times had averaged four seconds quicker than the winning go-cart.

It had been as humiliating as being excused from playing rugby. He'd had to watch in envy from the sidelines while Marcelo, the younger brother and therefore expendable, had barged his way through opposing players, sending them flying like bowling pins. But he'd swallowed that humiliation, lifted his chin proudly and cheered his brother on, just as he'd cheered on Sébastien, his number two.

'Dominic was guest of honour at a Grand Prix in France a few years ago,' she told him. Amadeo couldn't stop the curl of his lip at this nugget of information but strove not to let his revulsion at Dominic's name show on his face. 'He ignored his advisors and talked one of the teams into letting him drive their test car when the race was over. He crashed it.'

That brought a smile back to his face. 'Was he hurt?'

'Unfortunately, no.'

The deadpan way she'd said it made him laugh.

She giggled, but then the amusement died away and a softness came into her eyes. 'It is difficult, always having to go through life limited in what you can and can't do.'

'It is not something I should complain about,' he said dismissively. 'I have a very privileged life.' The strictures of his life were chains he had the freedom to break. No one would or could have physically stopped him from stepping onto the rugby pitch or getting into the go-cart, or prevented him following his dream into motor-racing. The only person who'd forced him to obey his parents' commands had been himself because he wanted what was best for the monarchy every bit as much as they did.

Amadeo had never been susceptible to emotions that would steer him away from his predestined path. Emotions had never controlled him, not even when he'd been a hormonal adolescent. Duty came first. Always.

It was duty that had led him to this point. Married to a woman he'd despised on sight. But he'd spent the entire meal alternating between fantasising about taking her on this dining table and searching for a sign that his growing desire for her was reciprocated.

Dio, how had he been so blind to how sexy she was? The way she ate was sexy. The tilt of her head. Even her composure was sexy. The thought of breaking that composure down until she lost complete control…

'You're still human,' she said.

If she could read his thoughts she'd discover just how human he was.

Dio, he wanted to lean across the table, gather the material of that sleeveless dress into a fist and pull her to him and kiss her so thoroughly she'd be unable to stand.

'Human, but not like other men.'

'If you were like other men you wouldn't be married to me,' she observed. 'And if I'd been born into a different family I wouldn't be married to you.'

Over a month of marriage and he'd never felt her tongue in his mouth. Never seen her naked.

'Who would you be married to if you were a different man of a different family and hadn't been obliged to make this marriage with me?' she asked, breaking into his erotic thoughts.

His mind went blank. The only face he could conjure was the woman swirling her wine glass opposite him. Her hair had dried during their meal. Ungroomed, it was wavier than he'd thought, cute flyaway curls springing out around her temples.

'I'm talking about your ideal woman if you could have chosen anyone,' she persisted. 'The fantasy of your imagination. Who would she be?'

'I don't have one.'

There was a slight narrowing of her eyes before a wry smile played on her plump lips. 'I think that might be the first lie you've told me.'

He scraped the last of the chocolate torte onto his spoon and hit her with a meaningful stare. 'A woman should only ask a man to reveal his fantasies if she's fully prepared for the answer.'

The stain that covered her cheeks reminded him that, until their marriage, Elsbeth had been a virgin. If she knew of all the erotic thoughts that had played through his head during their meal she would probably run out of the room screaming.

Or would she?

Was that a blush of embarrassment or indicative of something else?

Dio, he needed to strip that composure away and get her to open herself to him.

As tempting as it was to challenge her, ask her if she *really* wanted to know the female fantasy of his imagination, Elsbeth wasn't ready for his answer. She was too inexperienced.

Dabbing his mouth with his napkin, Amadeo rose to his feet. 'Time for bed.'

Elsbeth kept her chin up and her back straight as she walked the corridor to her bedroom. The twenty steps to reach the door took an eternity, as if she were in one of those crazy dreams where your destination was right in front of you but time itself had slowed down so much you couldn't reach it, every step the same step.

But she did reach it. And so did Amadeo. He'd walked silently beside her with an ease to his gait she had to fake to match.

Lord help her, she thought she really might throw up. She hadn't been this nervous on her wedding night. Nowhere near.

It was the deliberate way he'd thrown his napkin down and the decisive way he'd then stood. As if he'd come to a snap decision. Now was the time for sex!

She longed to believe the hunger she'd seen in his eyes throughout their meal had been real and not a figment of her needy imagination. She also longed for it not to be real, because if it was real then it was a false reality. How could a man with such an intense dislike of her and her family possibly want her?

But maybe she hadn't imagined it. Maybe he

did want her, maybe he was having one of those days her mother had warned her about when a man's testosterone levels rose and he became amorous. But Amadeo would never want *her*. She would always be the wife he'd been forced to marry, not the wife of his choosing. Not the wife of his fantasies, whoever that woman was. Whoever that woman was, she wasn't a Fernandez.

At their pre-wedding party she'd convinced herself Amadeo was the husband of her dreams. Those dreams had been ripped apart on their wedding night and she must not allow the craving her body felt for him dupe her into believing the impossible.

He was coming to her room for sex. Normal Duty sex. In an hour he'd be gone and everything would be as it should be.

The door closed.

She couldn't hear the silence through the blood drumming loudly in her head.

Now they were well and truly alone. Her maids wouldn't enter the room with Amadeo in it. They wouldn't even knock on the door to see if she needed them for anything.

They were well and truly alone and she didn't have a clue what she was supposed to do. The clock had turned back a month to their wedding night, when all she could do was wait for Amadeo to make his move.

His smooth voice broke through the whoosh-ing in her head.

'Would you mind if I used your shower?'

Surprised, she shook her head and forced her-self to meet his stare. 'Go ahead.'

His eyes glimmered and then, to her complete and utter shock, he brushed his lips against hers and murmured, 'I won't be long.'

Her mouth had barely registered the fleet-ing pressure and warmth before he nonchalantly strode away.

Feet rooted to the floor, lips tingling, heart pounding, Elsbeth watched him disappear into her bathroom. She pressed her trembling fingers to her mouth.

She was still standing there, feet rooted, fingers on lips, when the shower started up. That snapped her out of her trance, and she hurried to her ward-robe and grabbed the first nightdress on the pile. In seconds she'd yanked the maxi-dress and her knickers to the floor and shrugged the nightdress over her head. As her laundry basket was in the bathroom, she chucked her discarded clothes in the wardrobe, closed the door, then threw herself onto her dressing table seat.

Her naked face reflected back at her. Lord help her, her eyes look fevered, her skin flushed.

Elsbeth took ten deep breaths then reached for her cleanser.

She must stop reading too much into things.

So what if Amadeo was using her shower? It was more convenient than using her guest room like he'd done on their wedding night, which she was certain he'd only done so she could get ready in privacy. In that respect, he *had* been a gentleman. It was on her that she'd taken his consideration for her virgin nerves as a sign of romance.

The handle turned on the bathroom door.

The butterflies in her belly expanded their wings and became electrified.

Amadeo appeared with only a small towel around his waist.

One glance and inhalation was enough for her senses to be engulfed.

If the good Lord really had created Man in his own perfect image then that image would be Amadeo standing in the bathroom doorway in a cloud of steam, black hair damp, broad, tanned chest gleaming, as solid an example of the beauty of rampant masculinity as she'd ever witnessed.

How many times could a woman come close to spontaneously combusting in one evening?

Glimmering gaze on her, he padded to the bed. 'I hope you don't mind but I used the spare toothbrush in your vanity unit.'

She shook her head and rose to her feet. 'I don't mind at all. Excuse me a moment.'

Somehow she managed to force her feet to walk, not run, to the bathroom.

Amadeo watched Elsbeth slip gracefully into

the bathroom with narrowed eyes. Did he detect signs of fluster in her speech and movements? Or was he back in the realm of wishful thinking?

Sliding under the bedsheets, he propped himself against the velvet headboard.

There was a weight to his heartbeats he'd never felt before. He could only assume anticipation was the cause. It had been many years since excitement had reached its tentacles all the way to his core. His long-ago teenage years to be precise.

His decision to take a shower had been impulsively made when the bedroom door had closed behind them. Elsbeth wasn't used to preparing for bed with him around and, much as he'd fantasised about stripping her naked, he needed to keep his ardour in check if he wasn't going to frighten her.

He thought back to their first night together and how clinically satisfying it had been. Satisfying was no longer enough for him. He wanted fulfilling, and he wanted Elsbeth to be fulfilled and not merely satisfied too.

If he knew his wife, she'd go along with whatever he wanted. Yes, she'd go along with it but whether she'd take any enjoyment from it was unknown. He knew her, knew she had it in her head that her role in their marriage was to please him—probably the basest of all male fantasies but the most stomach-turning when applied to real life—but he couldn't read her.

How infuriating that the first woman he'd been

unable to read properly in his thirty-two years on this earth should be his wife.

There was movement behind the bathroom door.

Amadeo took a deep breath, stretched his neck and rolled his shoulders.

Elsbeth took one last deep breath for luck and opened the bathroom door.

Her heart slammed against her ribs to see Amadeo in bed waiting for her, a complete reversal of all the other nights they'd shared together. A half smile played on his sensual lips and he lifted the bedsheets off her side of the bed in invitation.

The short walk from bathroom to bed was the most excruciating taken in her life. With Amadeo's gaze openly on her, she didn't think she'd ever been so self-conscious, so aware of her naked breasts moving beneath the silk of the white nightdress.

She climbed onto the bed with all the elegance she could muster. No longer feeling she needed permission to turn her own bedside light off, she pressed the switch so only the dim light on Amadeo's side illuminated the room, lowered herself under the sheets and held her breath.

Now Amadeo would turn his light off. He would climb on top of her. He would kiss her. His hands would roam her body. His fingers would slide up her nightdress, discover she was ready for him—her body was her brain's ultimate betrayer—and then he would take her. He would hold his climax off until she'd had her climax—no one could say he wasn't a gentleman—and then, when they were both done, he would roll off her. If she was lucky, he would leave immediately and let her get on with self-soothing the gap their tender-less coupling left in her heart with his still-warm pillow.

She knew she was being unfair and making it seem as if they were two robots following a script when, during the act itself, she felt so much, but she needed to be unfair otherwise her growing need for more would grow *too* big and the rejection that underlay everything would bring her spiralling down.

Her brain accepted that Amadeo would never be her true lover. Their couplings had the sole purpose of making a baby. Now she just needed her body to accept it and stop responding to things that weren't there.

Amadeo stretched himself out next to her and settled onto his side. Propping himself on an elbow, he gazed down at Elsbeth's face. She was just so incredibly beautiful, from her big baby blue eyes to the snub nose and those lips that felt like marshmallow against his. He pressed a finger lightly to the centre of those lips and was rewarded with a widening of her eyes.

Gently, slowly, he trailed his finger to the edge of her mouth and then brushed it against the soft skin of her cheek. Not taking his eyes from hers, he brushed his fingers down the graceful neck to the shallow at the base he'd fantasised about touching earlier.

'Why do you wear these nightdresses for me when you wear shorts and T-shirt for yourself?' he murmured, now fingering the neck of her virgin nightdress, which skimmed across her collarbone.

Her eyes had darkened. Her breaths, when they came, were faint hitches he had to strain to hear. Her lips parted then pressed back together before she whispered, 'To please you.'

He skimmed over the swell of her breasts and encircled a tip that had hardened and strained against the white silk. 'Why would you think dressing like a sacrificial virgin would please me?'

She swallowed. 'My mother.'

His finger drifted over her flat belly, feeling almost imperceptible quivers. 'She told you that?'

She nodded. Colour flared across her delectable cheekbones.

Across her abdomen he drew to her hip, and down her thigh. 'What else did she tell you?'

Her always quiet voice was barely audible. 'Many things.'

He clasped the silk of her nightdress. 'Things to do with pleasing me?'

Another nod.

He gathered more material, sliding it up her

legs to the top of her thighs, stopping short of exposing her to him. 'Do you want to know what would please me now?'

A nod so small it was hardly there.

'What would please me most is if you took it off.'

CHAPTER NINE

ELSBETH'S HEART STOPPED beating at the impact of Amadeo's lazily delivered words.

Eyes hooded, he lowered his face closer to hers and her heart kick-started back to life, the beats so loud and fast they were nothing but a deafening burr.

'Will you let me see you the way I let you see me?' he whispered before dipping his face lower still so the tip of his nose brushed against her cheek and his warm breath melted into her skin. Her nightdress was now bunched at the top of her hips.

She was helpless to stop the quiver that rippled through the whole of her body, and groped desperately for coherent thought.

The palm of his hand slipped under the ruched silk and flattened against her back. Slowly he eased them both upright until Elsbeth sat facing him, trembling, the whooshing in her head a hot roar.

Fingers dragged through her hair, hooded green

eyes seeming to drink her in. He leaned in closer. Her breath caught in her throat and her eyes closed as his lips pressed against hers, as fleeting as the touch of a feather, his hands slowly moving down from the back of her head to her shoulders and down her sides to where her nightdress was gathered.

Pulling his face back, his eyes locked back onto hers and then, bit by bit, her nightdress was pushed over her belly and breasts. She lifted her arms. Silk fleetingly caressed her neck and face and then, for the first time in her life, Elsbeth was naked in front of a man, shaking, her heart beating so hard he must be able to see its ripples through her chest.

A finger gently lifted her chin.

She'd never been so scared of what she would find in Amadeo's gaze, terrified too of what she was feeling, how deeply her desire for him ran, trapped in every cell in every part of her body.

She forced herself to look at him. The dim glow of the bedside light cast his face in the shadows and plains that turned his features from mere drop-dead handsome to heart-breaking, and Elsbeth fought even harder to keep the essence of herself intact and not fall into the heady promise of the lie in his eyes, however desperately she wanted to believe the hunger she was reading in them was for her.

This was what her mother had warned her

about, the day when a man's ardour was stronger than normal.

When it was over, she would still sleep alone.

He palmed the flat of her back again and, with the same care as when he'd pulled her upright, lowered her back down so her head rested on her pillow. Then, with infinite care, he laid himself between her legs, elbows resting either side of her head, cocooning her with his body and the sheets he'd pulled up to his shoulders.

It was the romantic scene she'd longed for on her wedding night.

The weight of his erection brushed against the top of her thigh. The tips of her sensitised breasts brushed against his chest. Heaven help her, she had to make fists with her hands to temper herself against the craving to crush herself tightly against him.

For the longest time he said nothing, just gazed at her, his fingers smoothing her forehead. Desire was there, but something else too, as if he was trying to bore into the hidden caverns of her brain. It was a look that made her heart want to punch out of her chest and fly into his.

Don't fall, she begged herself, even as her body trembled at the tenderness of his touch. *It isn't real. Don't fall.*

His mouth closed in on hers. A feather-light kiss. Light, but with the power to send more thrills racing through her than all the other kisses they'd shared.

Another feather-light brush of his mouth.

Don't. Fall.

His lips fused against hers in the way they'd only ever done in her dreams, hard, demanding and yet so very sensual and, at the first flicker of his tongue against hers, the stray thoughts Elsbeth had managed to recapture and all the frantic warnings in her head flew away as heat and electricity crackled through to her core.

With a sigh of pleasure, she cupped the nape of his neck and melted into his mouth.

Amadeo shuddered at the scorch Elsbeth's light touch branded on his neck, and deepened the fusion of their mouths. Never had mere *kissing* been so potent, the clash of lips and tongues so erotic. What had he imagined? That to delve into a Fernandez's mouth would poison him? If there was poison it was soaked in nectar, an addictively sweet toxin that fed into his bloodstream and fed the hunger for her that had taken on a life of its own.

Her skin was laced with the same sweetness and, *Dio*, it was so soft, softer than brushed velvet, and he trailed his mouth and tongue down her brushed velvet neck into the shallow at the base that had so caught his fantasies.

He shifted lower, using his hands and mouth to explore her body. Even his wildest imagination couldn't have adequately conjured its beauty. Above her left breast sat a small mole he'd never seen before…he'd hardly seen *any* of her before. He kissed it before kissing lower still, over the swell of breasts so much fuller than he'd appreciated. Reverently, he took a hardened peak into his mouth, an electric thrill racing through him to finally hear the soft mew of Elsbeth's pleasure.

Forcing himself to keep his ardour in check, he lavished attention on each breast in turn, revelling in the subtle responses of her passion. It was all there, in the arch of her back, the delicate hitching of her breath, the familiar clenching of the bedsheets and the grazing of her right foot against the mattress.

More than that, he could *feel* it, the fevered heat consuming her, could feel it as deeply as the burn consuming him.

Flames were licking Elsbeth's skin. Every touch of Amadeo's hands, every brush of his body against hers, every lick of his tongue, every mark of his mouth burned through her flesh, melting her bones until she was nothing but a mass of pulsating need.

Who knew a tongue trailed in a circle around her navel could be so arousing, could send the flame burning even deeper? Nothing could have prepared her for such pleasure. She could lie there for ever, putty in the hands of this most hedonistic assault to her senses.

Putty in Amadeo's hands.

Those same hands were now holding her hips, his lips trailing down her abdomen. So lost in the sensations was she that when his mouth drew down her pubis she didn't realise what he intended until his tongue brushed against the place where her pleasure was always the most intense and sent a deep thrill rushing through her.

Reflexively, her heart thundering at both the unexpected action and the charge that rocketed through her, she pressed her thighs together.

Instinct told her this was a line of intimacy it was far too dangerous to cross.

But how could she say no to him? How many times had her mother told her that she must never say no to him about anything, that in the bedroom she was to take whatever he gave and give whatever he demanded?

She only realised Amadeo had stilled when his fingers suddenly bit deeper into the flesh of her hips and he kissed his way back up.

Had he guessed that she didn't want…?

He took a breast back into his mouth and her thoughts fragmented into dust.

One taste of heaven, that was all she'd allowed before clamping her thighs together. Just one little taste of a musky heat that had to be heaven-sent. The judder of her body at the first touch of his tongue… *Dio*, Amadeo had never known a reaction like it.

But she wasn't ready for it. As much as he longed to bury his face in her bliss and bring her to orgasm with his tongue, the freezing of her body told him it was too soon for her.

That was okay. He had the rest of his life to open her mind and her body to the hedonistic pleasures of the flesh.

Covering her with the entirety of his body, thrilling at the sensation of her naked breasts crushed against his chest, he gazed down, drinking in the shallowness of breaths through the parted lips swollen from his kisses, the flushed cheeks...

And then her eyes opened and locked onto his. What he found in them made the arousal he'd been containing through sheer will in his pursuit of her pleasure throb painfully.

It was a mirror of his own craving.

Dio, she was beautiful.

He kissed her. She moaned softly into his mouth and then he felt it, the light, almost tentative drag of her fingers over his back.

Breaking the kiss, the tip of his nose pressed to hers, Amadeo guided his arousal to the damp heat of her opening and almost lost his mind when she raised her thighs and pressed against him in, what was for his wife, a wanton invitation. In one long, slow thrust, he buried himself deep inside her, groaning loudly at the sheer heavenliness of it.

So this is what making love feels like...

Elsbeth cut the thought off. Whatever was happening to her, whatever ecstasy had been elicited under Amadeo's tender sensual assault, she must not fall into the trap of believing it had anything to do with love.

This, here, now, the *feelings*…

It was how she'd dreamed their wedding night would be.

Too late for that.

If this had been her wedding night she would have fallen in love with him.

Just hold onto yourself. Don't fall.

But it was so hard to hold on when their bodies were fused so tightly, Amadeo's muscles bunching beneath her touch, the taste of his mouth playing on her tongue and his groans of pleasure sinking into her ears.

All of her senses were filled with him.

She was slipping away from herself. The pleasure was just too intense to hold on. Wrapping her legs around his waist to deepen the penetration, she closed her eyes and submitted herself entirely to the heaven only Amadeo could take her to.

A strong hand clasped her bottom, lifting her only a touch, but a touch enough to tip her over the edge into ecstasy. Raising her head, she pressed her mouth into his neck and tightened her arms around him, breathing in the musky scent of his skin and tasting the salt on her tongue as the winding coil inside her shattered in an explosion of flickering light.

For the first time in his life, Amadeo didn't want to let go. This was just too good. Too...

Dio, he'd never felt anything like it. Ecstasy in every thrust. Ecstasy in every touch of her hand on his skin, in every kiss.

He didn't want to let go but he couldn't hold on any longer, not with Elsbeth's mouth so hot against his neck and the tight throbs of her climax dragging him so deep inside her he didn't know where she began and he ended, and the cries of her own ecstasy echoed in his ears.

Thrusting into her one last time, Amadeo submitted himself to the euphoria.

Elsbeth tried to breathe. Tried to gather her fragmented thoughts. Tried to stop her romantic heart attaching itself to the heart beating rapidly through the chest pressed so tightly against hers that they could be one.

How long had they lain there, her cheek in his neck, his ragged breaths hot in her hair?

She didn't know if she wanted to laugh or cry.

It had been beautiful. Everything she'd wished for on their wedding night.

For the first time in her life she'd felt cherished, but it was all a lie and at any moment Amadeo would roll off her, swing his legs off her bed and leave.

Even if she felt that she could ask him to stay, she wouldn't. She wouldn't be able to endure the rejection that would surely come.

And then it happened. His weight shifted off her and he rolled onto his back. Her heart shrivelled, opening up the hollow that always formed in the aftermath of their couplings.

Oh, why had he made it so *good*? Why had he acted as if he was making love to her when they both knew he despised her?

She tugged the sheets up over her breasts and folded her hands across her belly. It took a huge effort but she managed to drag air into her lungs, somehow breathing in a huge dose of Amadeo's scent and the scent of their lovemaking with it.

Stop thinking of it like that. It was only sex. Tender, beautiful sex.

Hot tears stabbed the back of her eyes and she squeezed them shut to stop them leaking. He'd be gone soon.

Amadeo, still trying to catch his breath, turned his face to Elsbeth. As usual, she was lying there placidly. It never ceased to amaze him how well she played dead after they came together. It was as if she switched a part of her brain off and disengaged with him entirely. Other than her shock on their first night when he'd told her about their living arrangements—and only then because she hadn't been expecting it—she gave the distinct impression that, his duty to procreation done, his presence in her bed was no longer required. Of course, she would never say it in words. Not the woman who'd been trained from birth to believe a wife's duty was to obey her husband. She never objected to anything.

How much of that playing dead was a mask, like the vacuous wind-up doll she'd portrayed? And if it was a mask, what was it hiding?

He couldn't understand why it plagued him to know what went on in the privacy of Elsbeth's head. It wasn't as if he actually *cared* what went on in there... Okay, he admitted, he did care, but only so far as he wanted to be satisfied that she wasn't unhappy. Any man would be the same. As his father had often said, an unhappy wife led to an unhappy life. He doubted he would ever be happy to have married her but, as he constantly had to remind himself, that wasn't her fault. Elsbeth's life before their marriage had been less than happy. He didn't want her misery within their marriage on his conscience, and that was the most infuriating thing because he couldn't read her mind or expressions to know when, if ever, she was unhappy about something. She was just too good at masking her true feelings.

Strictly, by the agreed rules and precedents already set between them, he should return to his quarters now, but there was something he needed to say before he could leave.

'What you said earlier about the nightdress and

your mother... Elsbeth, I don't know what advice she gave you before we married but I need you to believe—and I cannot stress this enough—that I am not your overlord. Your purpose in life is *not* to please me. I understand life here is different to what you're used to and that it's taking time for you to adjust, but I meant it when I said you don't owe me anything more than the obligations we have to each other and the monarchy. We both have a duty to present ourselves to the world in a manner that is fitting as members of the Berruti royal family...'

Something his adrenaline-fuelled, impetuous brother had spectacularly failed in when being photographed dangling from a helicopter tied to his rescued damsel in distress, his now-wife, Clara.

'...and behave in a manner that doesn't bring disgrace to our country, but what we do and how we behave within the privacy of the castle walls is down to personal choice, and that counts for both of us.'

That all said, Amadeo shifted over to the side of the bed and sat up. He was about to climb off the bed when Elsbeth quietly said, 'Amadeo, until I came here I was never given a choice. Not about anything. I was raised in a palace where men have complete control over women, and my father had complete control over me. The only time my permission was needed for something affecting me was for our marriage, and that was only because Gabriel insisted on it.'

Gabriel, Alessia's husband, the man who'd been tasked with negotiating the marriage. He'd refused to negotiate without Elsbeth's explicit consent.

'I didn't know how badly I wanted to leave until the opportunity came,' she added after a short silence. 'I would have agreed to marry anyone to get out of that palace. It's awful there, and things have got so much worse since Dominic took the throne. He's a bully and a narcissist. Everything has to revolve around him, and because he's cruel, others follow his lead and now there's a culture of cruelty and humiliation. He gets as much of a kick out of seeing others being cruel as he does being cruel himself.'

Amadeo, absorbing all this with a violent churning in his guts, twisted round to face her. 'How was he cruel to you?'

She shook her head. 'He wasn't. Not in the way he is to others. Dominic likes me. Or, should I say, he likes my silence and compliance. My father is his uncle and his closest advisor and confidant. I'm like a pet to him.' She gave a short bitter laugh. 'A cowering pet terrified it's going to be the next creature to get a kick. He chose me as your wife because, of all the eligible women in the House of Fernandez, I was considered the most meek and pliable and I was a virgin. Believe me, with my father, I never had the freedom to be anything *but* a virgin. In Dominic's eyes—and my father's—women are either whores or Madonnas, and all men want to marry the Madonnas. He assumed that's what you would want too, and assumed you would be grateful to be given such a highly prized asset.'

He felt sick.

But hadn't he known much of this? Hadn't Elsbeth's virginity been dangled before him with the same smug aplomb as if he'd been offered a mythical unicorn?

He'd known it but it hadn't struck him properly until now, with Elsbeth spelling it out to him.

Her chest rose and she breathed out slowly. 'My first memory is of my father slapping my mother's face for answering him back. I remember watching Dominic walk past Catalina and pinch her for fun. He was always hurting her. I dread to think what she would have suffered if she'd still lived in Monte Cleure when he took the throne.' The silk sheets twisted around her body rustled gently as she turned onto her side so that her whole body faced him. There was an intensity to her stare he'd never seen before. 'Please understand, the men have *all* the power there, and I always knew that, to survive, I needed to keep my mouth shut and obey. I've never been brave like my mother. She's strong and she's always protected me, and while I know now that many of the things she taught me are wrong for our marriage, she taught me them for the best of reasons. She had no reason to believe you would be any different to the royal men of Monte Cleure and I hardly dared hope for more either.'

Dio, his heart had expanded so much it was a struggle to open his throat to speak. 'But you do believe it now?' he whispered hoarsely. 'That I'm nothing like them?'

After the longest of pauses in which his whole body became suspended in dread, she nodded. 'I do believe it. It's just that old habits die hard, and I've spent twenty-four years thinking twice about every word I say and everything I do.'

Amadeo's relief was indescribable.

He wasn't perfect by any means. He could be impatient. Arrogant. Manipulative. Demanding. He was too aware of his royal dignity and became aggravated when not given proper deference. He was all those things and more, but he wasn't a bully. For sure, he'd demanded his brother and sister marry for the sake of the monarchy, but their marriages had both been a success so he'd been right to demand it of them, and he'd also done the same thing himself in marrying Elsbeth. Amadeo would never ask anyone to do anything he wasn't prepared to do himself. He wasn't a bully and he wasn't corrupt and he would sooner be burned at the stake than lay a finger on a woman.

She gave another laugh, this time with a more

genuine, if melancholic, ring to it. 'If Dominic or my father knew the attributes they prized the most in me were the things you hate most about me...' She laughed again, shaking her head.

'I don't hate you.' He didn't know what he felt for her, but hate it was not. Reaching for her hand, he brought it to his lips. 'Always remember, you have no obligation or duty to please or obey me. In the privacy of the castle walls, live how you want to live, dress how you want to dress, be free to say no to me and disagree with me and voice opinions and share your thoughts without fear of the consequences. I might not always like what you have to say but you might not always like what I have to say, and you shouldn't be afraid to say so.'

Elsbeth was helpless to stop her interlocked fingers from squeezing his or from searching the green eyes swirling with an emotion that terrified her, knowing if she stared long enough she could trick herself into believing that he cared. For her. When she knew it was impossible.

He wasn't heartless, but she already knew that. The truth about her life in the House of Fernandez had disturbed him, she'd seen it in the contortions of his face. His disgust at the situation there would be the same whoever had told it to him.

It came to her that she'd only confided the full truth because she trusted he wouldn't use it as a weapon to subjugate her, a threat like the bogeyman: *If you don't behave, you'll be sent back to Monte Cleure.*

What she couldn't do though, was trust her heart to him. Not when his heart was frozen to her.

'Thank you,' she whispered.

He shook his head, leaning in closer and matching the whisper of her voice. 'You have nothing to thank me for.'

Don't do this, she silently begged. *If you're going to leave then leave. Don't drag it out. Don't make it even harder for me.*

But her lips tingled at the whisper of his breath on them. The sigh of her heart had expanded into the hollow gap and, with it, lit the switch inside her so flickers of awareness zipped through cells still luxuriating in the sensations from just a short while ago, and deep inside her pelvis the flame reignited.

Hunger flared in the eyes gazing so intently into hers.

He was going to kiss her again.

Elsbeth swallowed the moisture that had filled her mouth. As badly as she ached to be gathered back into Amadeo's arms and experience all those glorious sensations again, at that moment her heart was too full and vulnerable to dare risk opening it even more to him. She needed to assert the freedom he'd just spelled out belonged to her and ask him to leave.

But then came the gentle fusion of his lips with hers and any thought of making him leave her bed flew away as she surrendered to the magic of his touch.

CHAPTER TEN

AMADEO WOKE WITH a start.

From the faint light seeping into the room, it was the cusp of morning.

He didn't remember turning his bedside light out.

Technically, it wasn't his bedside light. It was Elsbeth's. Because this was Elsbeth's bed in Elsbeth's room in Elsbeth's quarters. It was her warm body lying so close, her hip his hand was splayed on. Her rhythmic breathing the only sound in his ears.

There was a tightening in his guts as strong as the arousal in his loins. He didn't know where the tightening came from.

Making love to her a second time…

That hadn't been in the plan but he'd been caught in the moment.

The tightness eased as rationality returned. The rules set out before they had married and agreed with Elsbeth on their wedding night, had been separate quarters and separate personal lives. The other part of the agreement, spoken of and agreed privately between the two of them, had been to share her bed each Saturday until a child was conceived. Only by his own precedent had this been interpreted as him leaving straight after sex. Until the sun rose, it could still be interpreted as Saturday night rather than Sunday morning. But not for much longer.

It was time to return to his quarters.

Dio, extricating his body from hers felt like the hardest task in the world.

Careful not to wake her, he got out of bed and pulled his trousers on. Gathering the rest of his clothing, he took one last look at her before leaving the room.

Only when she heard the sound of the bedroom door closing did Elsbeth dare open her tear-filled eyes.

Oh, you silly fool. Why didn't you tell him to leave when you had the chance?

Swallowing back more tears, she reached for Amadeo's pillow and held it tightly to her chest.

Sébastien was explaining how his racing team had managed to achieve an average pitstop of two seconds. Usually, there was nothing Amadeo loved more than listening to his old school friend wax lyrical about his team's feats of engineering. As the motor racing calendar was on a two-week break, Sébastien's team were back in Ceres, testing and working hard to bring about all the incremental advantages that were the difference between first place and second.

Motor racing was a rules-based sport. Teams who flouted those rules could expect sanctions, and rightly so. Rules were the structure within which Amadeo lived his life. Without rules, systems were dismantled and anarchy given space to flourish. He'd obeyed the rule of not endangering his own life when he'd stepped aside all those years ago and let his number two take the wheel of the go-cart he'd taken the lead on engineering. Sébastien had been his number two.

It was possible he would have resented his friend if he'd used that race and the go-cart they'd created as a springboard to becoming a racing driver, but Sébastien was as clear-minded as Amadeo. He didn't have the talent to make it as a racing driver but he had the drive to create his own team. Amadeo had used some of his personal fortune to back that team and it had given him great satisfaction over the years watching them climb the ladder of success. Through his old friend and the team Sébastien commanded, Amadeo could live vicariously the path he would have taken had he not been born a prince.

Today though, Sébastien's words floated around him. They didn't penetrate. Amadeo's head was too full of the woman he'd left sleeping early that morning to allow anything else in. His veins were too full too, a lingering thrum of sensation a physical reminder of what they'd shared.

But what had they shared? he mockingly asked himself. Great sex? That was no reason to turn into a zombie. It had to be the things she'd confided in him about her life in Monte Cleure because, along with the constant image of Elsbeth's beautiful face in the throes of ecstasy, came fantasies of smacking his fist over and over into the King of Monte Cleure's nose.

It was just as well his family were only constitutional monarchs with no real power over their island, he reflected grimly. If power still resided in their hands, he would be tempted to call up the Ceres special forces and plot a way to topple the bastard.

King Dominic Fernandez was a monster with unlimited power.

But hadn't he already known the man was a monster, and known it long before he'd kidnapped Clara?

He'd known it but he'd been detached from it. The stories about Dominic had only been words. His loathing of the man had come from his own interactions with him over the years.

He didn't feel detached from it any more. Now his loathing felt personal.

He'd never had violent fantasies before. They

were as disturbing as the frequent urge to cut his day short and return straight to Elsbeth's bed.

Monday morning, and Amadeo stood at the stone balustrade of his balcony, coffee in hand, watching the sun rise.

The hairs on the nape of his neck rose before she appeared in the garden. Throat closing, he straightened, drinking in the sleep-tousled blonde hair and the short silk emerald robe covering whatever form of nightwear she had on. His loins thickened as he considered the possibility she wore nothing beneath it...

Did she sense his stare or had she come outside hopeful of seeing him? Whatever her reason, she'd barely trodden ten steps barefoot over the lawn when she turned her head.

Dio, the thump of his heart as their eyes clashed.

Was this why he'd come out onto his balcony so early? Was this why he'd woken even earlier than was usual for him? Had a part of him hoped to see her?

This was getting ridiculous. He hadn't thought making love on Saturday would rid him of the desire he felt for her but had assumed it would go some way to assuaging it. It wasn't supposed to have made things worse. He was acting like a lust-fuelled adolescent.

That lightened his mood. When he'd been a lust-fuelled adolescent, it hadn't taken long for his infatuations to pass, the objects of his desire nice and shiny for weeks at a time then the lustre fading until nothing was left and it was time to move on. He'd never allowed those temporary infatuations to control him even at their height.

His current infatuation with Elsbeth would fade too. It certainly wouldn't last. He supposed a certain limited affection that came from being so closely wound in other's orbit was to be expected. Sleeping in her bed hadn't broken any rules, only set a new precedent. His obsession was certainly no reason to break the rules of their marriage and invite her up to his quarters and into his bed on a non-agreed day. That only had the potential to complicate a situation that didn't need complicating.

Settled in his mind, he raised a hand in greeting.

Too much time passed before she raised a hand in return. More time stretched before he watched her slim shoulders rise and then she started walking back towards him.

Despite everything he'd just settled in his mind, his breath caught in his lungs. The closer she walked to the iron steps that would lead her up to his balcony, the harder his heart thumped.

But she didn't reach the steps. Instead, she disappeared from view into her own quarters.

It wasn't her mother's voice sternly telling her that a princess never made the first move—she knew it was futile to expect the shackles of her past to be thrown off overnight—that had stopped Elsbeth climbing the iron steps to Amadeo, and nor was it the agreement, made at Amadeo's instigation, of them leading separate lives within the castle walls. It wasn't even that after well over a month of marriage he hadn't invited her into his quarters that stopped her. It was the explosion in her heart at the mere sight of him.

The intensity of that explosion terrified her. These were feelings that had no place in their marriage and she needed to get a handle on them quickly. One night of beautiful sex, confidences and falling asleep in each other's arms did not change the fundamentals of her marriage. Just because Amadeo wanted her did not mean he wanted more from her. He'd proven that by creeping out of her bed without a whisper of goodbye and then spending Sunday at the racetrack. He hadn't even mentioned he was going, which only proved the fundamentals of their marriage hadn't changed.

It shouldn't hurt. But it did. Badly. And it was all her own fault for not asking him to leave her quarters when she'd known how vulnerable her heart had been to him at that time.

The meeting in the Queen's private offices that Wednesday to discuss the royal itinerary was the first family meeting Elsbeth had been invited to.

Her nerves at what, for her, was a momentous occasion, were quickly soothed by her mother-in-law's gracious welcome and her father-in-law's affectionate embrace. She'd seen little of them since the wedding and they were both keen to satisfy themselves that she'd settled into their family and that there was nothing she was unhappy about. Reassurances given, an invitation for a family meal the following week accepted, Elsbeth took her seat next to Amadeo at the huge oval table, and arranged her face. She could only pray he hadn't sensed the huge thump of her heart at the sight of him, and pray he couldn't hear its staccato beat, the tempo rising even higher as the cologne she so adored seeped into the air around her.

They led separate lives. They would always lead separate lives. Her brain accepted that. The sooner her heart accepted it too, the less vulnerable it would be to him.

'How have you enjoyed our break from engagements?' he asked while the others sat themselves down.

'Very well, thank you.' That was good. Her voice sounded normal. To her own ears, at least. She'd spent much of Monday with the castle's head gardener, brainstorming how to transform her and Amadeo's private garden into something resembling an English country garden, and then spent Tuesday reading books on the history of the castle. She'd found it fascinating. Unlike the palace she'd grown up in, which had been built entirely in King Albert's reign centuries before and then considered a masterpiece needing nothing more to be added, the Berrutis predominantly Gothic castle had evolved over a millennia, but especially in the centuries of the early medieval period, by a succession of monarchs determined to put their own individual stamp on it. She'd wondered briefly if Amadeo would want to put his own stamp on it too when he became King but then, because she was absolutely determined not to think about him on her few precious days without his company, wondered no more.

'And you?' she added. 'Did you enjoy your day at the racetrack on Sunday?'

If he was surprised that she knew where he'd spent the day, he didn't show it. As she was coming to learn, nothing stayed secret for long in the castle. Gossip seeped through the draughts in the old stone walls or, in her case, through the mouths of her staff.

'I did, thank you.'

Queen Isabella's private secretary, who outranked all the other private secretaries, called for order, and the meeting got underway.

Since when had he come to like Elsbeth's perfume? Amadeo wondered. From the moment she'd taken the seat beside his, her delicate scent had swirled gently around him, and he was having to stop himself from greedily inhaling it deep into his lungs. To make things worse, he was wholly aware of the closeness of her body next to his too, and couldn't seem to stop his stare dipping down to the pretty hands folded neatly on the table and willing them to place themselves onto his lap.

It was one thing having lazy fantasies about her when they were being transported to and from engagements, quite another to fight flickers of arousal in the middle of an important family conference. How many times had he reproached his siblings for not contributing enough to these meetings over the years? And how often in the short time Clara had been in their lives had he bitten back words of censure over her tendency to get visibly bored and fidget her way through them?

Leaning his body away from Elsbeth, he gritted his teeth and forced his concentration onto the topic of planned state visits for the following year, and joined in the arguments with his family over who should and should not take each one. Unsurprisingly, everyone thought they were best placed to do the week-long visit to the Caribbean island of Bandhi, which would be celebrating its two-hundredth year of independence. Marcelo and Alessia, having worn their parents down, were on the verge of tossing a coin for it when his eyes, unbidden by his brain, glanced at Elsbeth.

His heart throbbed at the concentration on her face. How silently she sat there, trying her best to keep up with their language. They weren't making it easy for her, he acknowledged, not with them all talking over each other, all efforts to speak slowly so the non-native speakers could keep up forgotten.

If anyone deserved a week in the Caribbean, it was Elsbeth. That thought was all he needed to pull rank and nab that state visit for himself.

Ignoring his brother and sister's outraged faces, he quickly filled Elsbeth in and was gratified at the spark of excitement that flashed in her eyes before she turned her attention back to concentrating on the next argument. This one involved who didn't want to travel to a country renowned for its year-round atrocious weather.

Another hour passed before the meeting wound up but, before they could rise from their seats, his mother removed her reading glasses and looked at her three children in turn. 'There is one more item of business to discuss before everyone leaves. The King of Monte Cleure has announced his plans to attend next month's Grand Prix—'

'Here in Ceres?' Amadeo interrupted sharply.

Her eyes met his with equal sharpness. 'Yes. As we're all aware, protocol dictates that we should offer him our hospitality.'

Both Amadeo and Marcelo snapped, 'No,' in unison.

Their mother was tiny, barely touching four foot ten, a good foot and a half shorter than her two sons, but what she lacked in height, she made up for in stature. Fixing them both with a glare, she said, 'I appreciate that feelings concerning that man run high but need I remind you both that you each married to prevent a trade and diplomatic war between our two countries? Failure to give due hospitality could be seen as provocation by him and then we could find ourselves back to where we were and our country and monarchy threatened.'

'I don't want that animal within a hundred kilometres of Clara,' Marcelo said flatly. 'We hosted him for Amadeo's wedding and that ridiculous pre-wedding party. We've done our bit.'

With steel in her voice, their mother said, 'I've already had my team invite him to stay here at the castle. He will fly in on the Sunday morning and go directly to the racetrack. After the race he will return to the castle as our honoured guest and attend the banquet we're hosting, and then fly home the next morning. We will only have to suffer his presence for the one night.' Then she looked directly at Clara, who Marcelo had been furiously translating for, and said in slow English, 'I am sorry. I know it is hard for you.'

Clara shrugged. 'I understand.' Then she grinned. 'I'll try not to accidentally stab him.'

'I'll try not to stab him too,' Alessia chirped up.

'What about you, Elsbeth?' Clara asked with a cackle of laughter. 'Are you going to try not to stab him too?'

As soon as the meeting was over, Elsbeth's arm was taken by Amadeo and she was steered into an empty office.

He looked frazzled. As impeccably groomed as

he always was, there was a wildness in his eyes she'd never seen before. 'Did you understand all that?'

'About Dominic coming to Ceres?' she guessed.

He nodded tersely. 'The plan is for him to come for the Grand Prix and then attend the banquet we host each year for the race teams and their families, and stay for the night as our honoured guest.'

He practically spat the last three words out.

'I thought that's what you were all saying.'

'Say the word and I'll put a stop to it.'

Touched, she smiled. 'You don't have to do that. Not for me. If Clara can cope with him being here then I can too. After all, isn't harmony between our two nations the whole reason you married me?' She needed to say that more to remind herself than him because the way he was looking at her…

There was something about the wildness of his stare that made her think of dragon-slaying heroes of old.

It was on the tip of Amadeo's tongue to say it was the whole reason she'd married him too, but his conscience stepped in and stopped him. His conscience knew it would be a lie.

Elsbeth had married him because she'd had no choice. Not any real choice. Was it any wonder she dressed for bed as a sacrificial virgin when, in essence, that was exactly what she'd been? How free a choice was it to marry someone when the alternative was more subjugation?

Dominic and her father had sold her to the highest bidder. And that bidder had been him.

It was his conscience's good fortune that she held a genuine attraction to him and that she was happy here in her new life. God knew she'd not had much in the way of happiness before she'd come here.

'I will keep him away from you,' he vowed.

Taking his hand in hers, she squeezed it and said softly, 'Truly, there's no need. Dominic's never hurt me before, not like the others, and, even if he had, he's not stupid enough to try anything with an audience of hundreds. Don't ruin everything you and Marcelo and Alessia have achieved through your marriages out of anger. He's not worth it.'

And then her gaze lowered to their joined hands and, a hint of colour staining her cheeks, she let go and took a step back, her fingers grabbing at the skirt of her long, pretty, modest dress.

His fingers still burned from her touch.

Her eyes lifted back to his. Her chest made the tiniest, almost imperceptible hitch.

The strangest, tensest silence swirled and grew. The urge to push her against the nearest wall and work off the anger infecting him in the sweetness of her kisses grew with it. *Dio*, look at those lips. Did anything on this earth taste as sweet?

He closed the space she'd made.

Her chest hitched again, her graceful neck elongating then moving as if she were swallowing. Her eyes darkened, the colour on her cheeks deepening.

He leaned in, unable to look at anything now but those divine lips, moisture filling his mouth in anticipation of his hunger being sated...

The office door opened and a press secretary walked in. 'My apologies,' he said, clearly startled at who he'd found hiding there.

Amadeo took a step back and resisted the urge to throw the man out of his own office. 'No need for apologies,' he said with all the smoothness he could muster.

Holding the door open for Elsbeth, she walked past him, causing another waft of her beautiful perfume to envelop him like a cloud.

The urge to snatch her hand into his and drag her straight to the nearest bed was strong. Too strong.

Everything he was feeling at that moment was too strong.

'I'm going to the gym,' he told her in as even a voice as he could manage when they reached their shared reception room.

There were agreed rules about their marriage. Good rules. Sensible rules. He should know—he'd imposed them. He would not break them for something as fleeting as lust. Their marriage was working perfectly well. Better than he could have hoped. They had achieved a cordiality he'd never believed he would find with a Fernandez.

But the dazed sheen he found in her eyes when she looked back at him made him come within a whisker of saying to hell with those rules and to hell with doing something as insipid as snatching her hand, and just throwing her over his shoulder, kicking her front door down and carrying her off to bed.

It was also that dazed sheen that stopped him following his baser instincts.

Elsbeth's heart was tender, that was becoming clearer the more time they spent together. He would do whatever he could to make her life here a happy one, and the state trip to the Caribbean was only the start. But what he would not do was let her believe their marriage could be anything more than what came within the bounds of the rules they'd agreed.

CHAPTER ELEVEN

ELSBETH HAD NEVER known time to pass as slowly as it did over the next few days.

Two days of engagements crawled at the rate of a lethargic snail. All she could think of was Amadeo. Spending hours with him, much of that time in a car, didn't help. It didn't matter how hard she tried to maintain her composure and indifference, the burn of his eyes on her skin was too much. And the burn was constant. Every time she caught his stare, he stripped her naked with his eyes. Every time she caught his stare, her bones melted.

Amadeo had lit something within her during their last night together, stoked it in those mad moments in the secretary's office when she'd been so *certain* he was going to kiss her, and she didn't have a clue how to extinguish it or control it.

Who cared about protecting her heart when she could barely walk for desire? She wished he had kissed her and whisked her off somewhere to make love to her again. Maybe then the heat that had bubbled incessantly since would have been sated instead of being allowed to simmer. And it had simmered every second of every minute of every hour.

Now it was two a.m. and she was wide awake, her heart still refusing to settle and her pelvis feeling as if it was on fire.

Saturday had finally come.

Tonight he would make love to her again.

She willed time to speed up.

By the time Saturday finally dawned, Amadeo felt like a tinderbox with a lit taper slowly crawling towards it.

As soon as he woke, he pulled on a pair of jeans and headed out to his balcony. Ten minutes of waiting and no sign of Elsbeth in the garden.

Where was she? Every morning that week he'd stood at the French doors of his balcony and watched her walk across the lawn of their garden. A warning voice had told him to stay hidden, take a little private fix of her beauty and then get on with his day.

Since that moment in the press secretary's office, getting on with his day had become a titanic battle with himself. He *burned* with unfulfilled desire. Burned. That perfume he'd so detested... now he couldn't get enough of it. Now, when they travelled to and from their engagements, every inhalation came with a dose of it, and it shot straight to his loins. *Dio*, it had been bad enough before, sitting in an enclosed space with the object of his infatuation there, close enough to touch, but now...

He could not believe the strength of his craving for her.

And she wanted him too. It had been written all over her face in that mad moment. As still as she held herself and as indifferent her outward body language during the hours they'd spent on engagements the last two days, she could no longer mask her eyes to him, or mask the desire they contained. That composure she wore like an iron cloak...slowly but surely it was slipping off her shoulders. He ached to rip it away and watch her lose the last of her control, and then bury himself in her.

Impulse took possession of him.

Not bothering to put a T-shirt on or anything on his feet, Amadeo bounded down the iron steps from his balcony and knocked loudly on her French doors.

He gave her ten seconds and knocked again. And again.

A shadow appeared through the glass before the door opened. Instead of Elsbeth, he was confronted with an armed palace guard, who took one look at him, turned bright red and set off with a profusion of apologies.

'It's okay,' Amadeo said, interrupting him impatiently once he'd got the gist that the guard had been stationed in his and Elsbeth's joint reception room and, when he'd heard unexpected banging on the French door at six in the morning, had done what he was trained to do. 'It's great that you're so alert and doing your job so well and keeping the Princess safe. Where is she?'

'In her room with Gregor.' Gregor was the other guard.

'Good man. You can return to your post. Radio Gregor and give him the all-clear.'

Striding through the day room—a deep red armchair had been added to it, replacing, he was sure, a dusky pink one—he then turned into the corridor at the same moment Gregor left Elsbeth's room, speaking into the walkie-talkie the guards used to communicate when stationed on duty. Behind him, Elsbeth appeared, wearing a short black nightdress that perfectly showed off the delectable golden legs he'd so admired from his balcony.

She came to a sudden halt.

Eyes puffy from sleep captured his, a light forming in them as her chest rose.

He stepped closer to her. *Dio*, in this sleepy tousle-haired state she really did look good enough to eat.

'I thought you were an early riser,' he murmured.

Her throat moved a number of times before she whispered, 'I had trouble falling asleep.'

Standing before her, he gazed deep into her eyes. 'And why is that?'

The colour staining her cheeks was a joy to witness, and he knew, without a solitary shadow of doubt, that what had kept her from sleeping was the same thing that had woken him before the sun.

Saturday. Their day.

She'd been waiting for it with the same heightened expectation as he had.

They had all day if they wanted. No rules would be broken.

A whole day to sate their hunger.

His arousal, finally freed from the mental chains he'd kept it clamped in for days, throbbed and burned.

He reached for her.

Elsbeth couldn't move. She was spent. Her limbs were jelly, her pelvis tingling, molten.

Amadeo was still inside her, his face buried in her hair, his breathing ragged.

She couldn't believe what had just happened. How it had felt to have her husband take her in his arms and practically throw her on the bed in his passion for her.

It had been like waking from the most wonderful dream, only to find the dream was real.

But now he raised his head and some instinct for self-preservation stirred within her, and she tried desperately to prepare herself for what came next and fought with equal desperation not to open her mouth and beg him to stay.

Instead of moving off her, he gazed down at her. He didn't say anything for the longest time, just stared at her before a half-smile formed on the lips that had kissed her with such fervour her mouth still buzzed. 'Breakfast in bed?'

Relief that he wasn't planning to leave straight away punched through her with such strength that she couldn't find the words to speak, could only nod.

'Good, I'm ravenous.' His eyes gleamed as he lifted his weight off her. 'Let's take a shower together while we wait.'

Her insides froze.

All their lovemaking took place under the protective cover of her bedsheets. She was exposed to him but the magical things he did to her overrode her shyness.

To shower with him? Her nudity on full display under the bright bathroom lights?

A week ago, she would have obeyed without question. She would have hidden her fear and gone along with it to please him.

You have no obligation or duty to please or obey me…

She had to swallow hard to loosen the constriction in her throat before she could speak. 'I don't think I'm ready for that.'

He stared at her with that look that always felt

as if he was trying to probe into her head, then smiled and gave a nonchalant shrug. 'No problem. Do you want to shower first or shall I?'

'I'm sorry.'

He captured her chin in his hand and brought his face to hers. 'Never apologise for saying no. You first or me?'

'You.'

'Then you can order the food. Tell the kitchen I'll have my usual.'

The relief this time was so overwhelming that her heart calmed. Palming his cheek, she whispered, 'Thank you.'

He kissed her palm and then kissed her mouth before jumping off the bed.

With the unashamed indifference to his own nudity she was coming to know so well, he strolled to the bathroom.

Shortly, the sound of running water started.

Elsbeth closed her eyes and placed the palm his lips had just kissed to her thrashing heart.

Breakfast was brought to Elsbeth's bedroom. Dressed only in her silk robe, Amadeo wearing only a towel around his waist, they sat on a wide chaise longue in the corner of the room, Amadeo peppering her with questions about her plans for their garden. It seemed surreal that it was still early morning. Surreal that she was sharing breakfast with her husband and that it felt so right.

She really was starting to think of him as her husband. To feel it too. What she was trying not to do was feel possessive about him, feel as though he was hers. He would never belong to her. Not where it mattered most, with his heart...

Or was she being too cynical? After all, there had been significant changes in his attitude towards her since their marriage. She no longer felt any kind of antipathy from him, no longer felt that she irritated him. Slowly but surely they were building an accord that didn't just include mind-blowing sex but also a form of friendship.

Was it possible that his heart could be opening to her as her heart was opening to him? She no longer sensed loathing from him, but it was foolish to even hope. Best to enjoy the time they shared together for what it was and what it gave her, and not leave her heart even more vulnerable by daring to dream for more.

'You know what we were talking about last week, about your mother?' Amadeo said when she'd finished enthusing about the plants and flowers she intended to grow and the huge greenhouse that was being built for her. The animation on her pretty face had been fascinating. He thought back to the frightened, shy stranger of six weeks ago—not that he'd recognised her fear and shyness for what they were back then—and was awed at her growing confidence. He remembered the first time he'd seen the animated side of her nature, that evening when she'd explained why she'd replaced a masterpiece with a school-girl's amateur painting. It had been the first time a hint of the real Elsbeth had shone through the wind-up doll persona she'd hidden herself behind.

But not all her barriers had been dismantled. The cloak hadn't slipped off in its entirety.

There was a passionate, sensual woman in there fighting to be released. He could feel that woman when he made love to her, ardent in her responses to him but always holding something back, frightened to take that last step and truly release the shackles her upbringing had placed around her and throw the cloak away. Embrace her sexuality.

Her cup of tea at her mouth, her pretty eyebrows drew together in question.

'About you pleasing me,' he reminded her. 'She told you to always please me in bed?'

Her cheeks coloured prettily and she nodded.

'What did she say?'

She lowered the cup from her mouth, the colour on her face darkening as she quietly said, 'That a prince's wife is a vessel for his pleasure.'

'Lie back, close your eyes, think of Monte Cleure and let me do what I want to you?'

He didn't think he'd ever seen such a flame cover her face, but she didn't drop her stare from his. 'Yes.'

'She never told you that you should expect pleasure too?'

'She said some women were lucky enough to receive pleasure from their husbands, but that I shouldn't expect it or ask for it.' She put her cup back on the saucer, her cheeks now scarlet as a contortion of expressions flittered over her face.

He removed the clattering cup and saucer from her, placed it on the antique coffee table the rest of their breakfast stuff was spread out on, and idly asked, 'Have you ever given yourself pleasure?'

Eyes widening in shock, her hands flew to her cheeks and she shook her head shakily.

'Don't be embarrassed,' he murmured, leaning into her. 'And do not be ashamed. Pleasure isn't shameful.' He captured the sash around her waist and untied it one-handed. 'Asking for pleasure isn't shameful…' He bent his head to capture a puckered nipple in his mouth, heard the short, soft mew. 'But to truly know what gives you the most pleasure you need to understand the basics of what works for you.' Loosening the towel around his waist, he kissed his way up to her mouth and stretched out on his side beside her.

Her eyes didn't leave his face, not even when he reached for a trembling hand and placed it on her pubis, nor when he took hold of his erection.

Slowly, he moved his hand up and down his arousal. Voice thickening, he leaned his face closer to hers. 'Do you see what I'm doing? There is nothing wrong with self-pleasure. It's how we learn best.'

Elsbeth felt almost drugged with arousal. It was the sensuality in Amadeo's voice…the heat in his eyes. She was almost afraid to look at what he was doing to himself.

Breathing raggedly, she lifted her head and…

Dear Lord…

He was masturbating. His gaze was fixed on her and he was masturbating.

'You don't have to touch yourself,' he whispered thickly. 'You don't have to do anything. If this makes you uncomfortable and you want me to stop then I will stop. Do you want me to stop?'

Her head shook itself.

His mouth hovered over hers. 'Does it excite you?'

Excite her? She'd never seen anything so erotic in her life as her giant, sexy husband pleasuring himself. She'd never *dreamed* she would find such a sight erotic.

Her heart thumping, skin inflamed, she tiptoed her fingers down to her slickness. Her index finger slipped over her swollen sex and she gasped at the shock of excitement.

He groaned. '*Mio dio*, you're so sexy.'

She touched the swollen spot that all her pleasure emanated from again, and this time she kept her hand there.

The pleasure…*heavens*. So different to how it felt when Amadeo was inside her and yet, with that hooded, burning look in his eyes, somehow even more intimate. She'd never imagined he would look at her the way he was now. As if he could stare at her for a thousand years and still want to look some more.

'*Dio*, you have no idea how badly I want to taste you,' he muttered.

'Then do it.'

Was that *her* voice? It didn't sound like her voice, but the words came from her mouth.

And that didn't feel like her quivering body his lips caressed as he snaked his way down it, but the sensation was everywhere, a heavy, dazzling cloud embracing her, making her head spin.

At the first press of his tongue to the place she most craved it, her thoughts dissolved into the cloud. When the lightning hit, its strength made her cry out as she shattered into a billion pieces.

Elsbeth opened her eyes and her heart twisted with sadness. At some point since they'd last made love, the room had darkened. Night was falling.

At some point soon, Amadeo would leave. The weight of his arm over her belly and the leg entwined with hers would leave with him. The mouth pressed into her hair. It would all be gone.

The most magical day of her life would come to an end.

But at least she'd experienced it. She'd had this

day of utter, heady bliss, and that could never be taken from her. She would treasure it always.

She wished she could tell her mother how wrong she'd been, but that would be cruel. Unless something happened to Dominic, like an uprising or a personality transplant, her mother would never be allowed to leave her father. She would never know the delights that could be found in a man's touch. The joy. The hedonism. The effects more potent than the finest champagne and, she suspected, more addictive than any narcotic.

She had no idea how she could continue to protect her heart after the day they'd just shared. She didn't see how it was possible.

As all these thoughts played in her head, she became aware of a heaviness forming in her abdomen. Holding her breath, she concentrated hard on it but then let out a muted gasp as a cramp fisted in her.

Oh, no. No. Please, no.

The heaviness spread. Another cramp came. Not as sharp or as powerful as the ones she'd always had before the medication she'd been given to tame it, but unmistakable all the same.

She breathed in deeply and carefully disentangled herself from Amadeo's sleeping form.

In the bathroom, she took some painkillers then stepped into the shower.

As the hot water sprayed over her head and

body, she let the tears fall. Only when the tears had turned themselves off did she turn the shower off.

Wrapping a towel around herself, she wiped the steamed-up mirror. Her unhappiness reflected back at her.

The best day of her life given the worst possible finale.

Amadeo was awake and sitting up propped against the headboard when she walked back into the bedroom wearing clean pyjamas. The hungry, welcoming smile faded as he looked at her.

'I wondered what was taking you so long,' he said before giving a rueful smile. 'It is that time?'

She nodded, afraid she might start crying again. She didn't even know why she'd cried to begin with. When the doctor had seen her about her menstrual pains, she'd asked how long it would take to conceive. He'd told her it could take many months and that for some couples it took years.

He pulled the sheets back and patted the space beside him, and suddenly, with that gesture alone, her tears made perfect sense.

She'd been convinced the fact of her period would mean Amadeo had no reason to stay. She'd been afraid he would take it as his cue to leave.

She didn't want him to go.

Climbing onto the bed, she sank into the comfort of his arms and the strength of his masculine body and wished with all her heart that this didn't feel so right.

Leaving a bed had never been so difficult.

Amadeo hadn't planned to spend the whole night with her again. But then, he hadn't planned to spend a whole day making love to her. *Dio*, he couldn't get enough of her. Elsbeth was the most intoxicating aphrodisiac in the world.

He'd never had a day like it. An entire day devoted to nothing but pleasure. He could do it all again, starting right now. Press a kiss into that sensitive spot on her neck that he'd discovered and...

He took a deep breath and willed the surge of lust-driven adrenalin to abate. It wasn't just that it was the time of month when he couldn't make love to her that made him sever his amorous thoughts. The sun was rising. A new day was dawning. Their day and night together was over.

He placed a gentle kiss to her temple.

Her eyes flew open.

A weight lodged in his heart. 'I need to go now.'

She nodded.

'I...' It was on the tip of his tongue to invite her to share lunch with him. And dinner. 'I'll see you soon.'

Another nod.

Damn it. One swift, hard kiss to her mouth and then he left.

Climbing the stairs to his quarters, it felt as if the weight that had attached itself to his heart had a pendulum attached to it.

Elsbeth hugged his pillow tightly to her chest but there were no tears.

Amadeo had stayed the whole night with her. He'd kissed her goodbye. And she'd seen it in his eyes. He hadn't wanted to leave.

Dare she hope...dare she...that his feelings were changing in the same way that hers were?

CHAPTER TWELVE

ELSBETH DID NOT think she'd ever been as excited as she was when getting ready the following Saturday. She hadn't been this excited on her wedding day—there had been too much fear of the unknown mixed in with the excitement back then to compare.

They were going to a party. A proper party, not a royal engagement, hosted by a billionaire friend of Amadeo's who'd recently bought a street in one of the most affluent parts of Ceres' capital and knocked it into one big home for himself, and now wanted to show it off. A proper, social party. Even better, Clara and Marcelo, and Alessia and Gabriel were going too. It was rare for Amadeo's sister and brother-in-law to be in Ceres over weekends, preferring to spend their free time at Gabriel's Madrid home, but for this occasion they'd decided to stay at the castle and party with the rest of them.

Elsbeth knew Alessia and Clara had been friends for many years. Their history and closeness could easily make Elsbeth the spare wheel but the few times the three of them had spent time together, they'd gone out of their way to make her feel that she was one of them. That she belonged. It was a wonderful feeling. Acceptance. They'd been like that on Tuesday evening at the family dinner the King and Queen had hosted. Clara had downloaded an app that translated everything spoken into the phone and had insisted Elsbeth and Alessia do the same, then spent the rest of the evening narrating dirty jokes in English and cackling with glee as it was translated by monotone voices in their own languages. Elsbeth had laughed so hard that in the morning her ribs had felt bruised.

The best part about Tuesday evening though, had been Amadeo. She'd never seen her stiff-necked husband so relaxed, not outside the privacy of their bedroom. Her bedroom. When, after the meal, they'd returned to their shared reception room and they'd turned to each other to say goodnight...

To remember the look that had been in his eyes was enough to make her bones go weak.

To remember the groan of disappointment he hadn't been quick enough to stifle in its entirety when she'd had to tell him her period hadn't finished and the last, rueful look he'd given her as he'd trudged up the stairs to his quarters was enough to make her heart sing.

He'd been on the verge of breaking the rules. She knew it as clearly as she knew her own name.

The next morning, he'd casually asked if she would like to accompany him for a meal with the Italian ambassador and her husband on Friday evening. Equally casually, she'd said yes. They'd returned to the castle at midnight. They'd barely made it through the door before he'd started ripping her clothes off. She'd woken with the rising sun to the most beautiful climax then fallen back asleep in his arms. He'd left her bed two hours ago.

The beautician who'd now finished drying her hair carefully gathered it together, a finger lightly touching Elsbeth's neck. She shivered, her mind racing ahead to their return from the party, when Amadeo would return to her bed.

God, she was starting to live for his lovemaking. She simply couldn't get enough of it.

She thought back to the shy bride who'd been so desperate to leave her home country she would have agreed to live in a pigsty. She remembered the naive virgin who'd believed she had to lie on her back and think of Monte Cleure. How apprehensive she'd been. How rigidly she'd held herself, believing her mother's advice not to touch him unless told. Believing that his pleasure was the only thing that counted, her own reactions to his touch and the climax he always brought her to a delightful bonus.

That shy, innocent bride would never have believed she would wake in the night aching so badly for him that she would bring herself to a climax with images of the time Amadeo had taught her *how* to bring herself pleasure behind her closed eyes. But as satisfactory as the solo climax had been, it hadn't been enough. It wasn't the same without him. Not even close.

That shy bride had gone. The rules her mother had drilled into her had no place here, and it was with this thought that she saw the dress she'd earmarked to wear that night hanging up, ready to be slipped over her head. A pretty, modest dress. As pretty and modest as everything she'd ever worn her entire life.

Not all the shackles of her past had been broken yet. Tonight it was time to smash another one.

Amadeo paced Elsbeth's day room, the glass in his hand filled with scotch from the bottle that had sat in her bar since the last time he'd drunk from it all those weeks ago. The night his loathing of his wife had first softened.

He would never have believed then that a time would come when he'd pace her quarters to stop himself marching down the corridor to her bedroom so he could throw her on the bed. If she were alone he wouldn't think twice, but she had an army of beauticians working on her—unnecessarily in his opinion. Elsbeth's beauty was innate.

She didn't need any help. But, as he was a stickler for rules himself, he had to allow when others had rules they abided by, and for the women of the Berruti family that meant spending hours being pampered and beautified before an evening out. In this case though, he considered it a waste of valuable sex time.

Pouring himself another drink, he thought moodily back to Tuesday evening, when he'd come within a whisker of sweeping her into his arms. All that had stopped him was her rueful explanation that her period hadn't finished. Unlike that day in the press secretary's office, he knew he wouldn't have stopped himself.

That was what came of spending an evening sitting next to his wife with the scent of her perfume arousing his senses and the heat from her hot body so close to his, arousing his loins. It got to the stage where a man would throw aside every rule invented just for one taste of his wife's sweetness.

Mother Nature had had other ideas though. A cold shower had done nothing to ease his ardour and so he'd resorted to masturbation, Elsbeth's face as she climaxed and the soft mews she made vivid in his memories as he'd brought himself to orgasm. But it hadn't been enough. As satisfactory as masturbation was, it didn't compare. Nothing could compare with the rapture of climaxing buried deep in Elsbeth's velvet tightness.

Dio, when would this fever for her be spent?

Maybe he should arrange a week away for them. That wouldn't be against the rules. The rules of their sleeping arrangements only applied in the castle. He could whisk her away to the Berrutis' villa in the Seychelles and make love until neither of them could walk and the fever had broken.

There were no spaces in his schedule for a week away until the New Year.

This fever had to be spent by then. It had to.

He'd just tipped half his refilled glass into his mouth when there was movement at the door. His heart thumped so hard its kicking beat rippled into every part of him.

Unable to speak, he could only stare and strive for breath.

Gone were the muted colours and modest cut Elsbeth usually wore, her dress a strapless deep red with gold embroidery lacing through the tight bodice and through the flared skirt that became pure lace from mid-thigh to ankle. Her bare slender legs shimmered through it, on her feet high black criss-cross sandals that elongated her shapely body. Her light blonde hair was twisted into an elegant bun at the nape of her neck, her only jewellery her wedding ring and gold hooped earrings, leaving nothing between the curve of her neck and the creamy hint of cleavage. Minimal make-up adorned the face that needed no embellishment...apart from her mouth. Elsbeth's plump lips, usually painted a soft pink, were painted red to match her dress. Dragging his gaze down her a second time, he noted dimly her finger and toenails were painted the same hue.

The whole effect was electrifying.

A strong buzz thrummed through his veins, visions of pressing her back through the door and backing her to the nearest wall, yanking that dress up to her waist and—

Still fighting for breath, he scoured the image from his mind. Tried to scour it.

Mio dio.

This was his wife?

A warm glow fired in Elsbeth's belly at Amadeo's reaction. Not that there was much in the way of a reaction, not in the physical sense. But it was there in the hooded glimmer of his eyes and the subtle flare of his nostrils, and it sent a thrill rushing through her.

She hadn't had the last-minute change of mind about her dress for Amadeo. She'd changed her mind for *her*, the dress having hung behind the panelling of her room in the hidden wardrobe since the designer had made it for her all those weeks ago. She'd fingered the delicate lace many times, wistfully thinking she would never find the courage to wear it, the image of her mother's disapproval too strong.

But she wasn't Lady Elsbeth Fernandez of the royal House of Fernandez of Monte Cleure any more. She was Princess Elsbeth Berruti of

Ceres. A princess of Ceres could wear whatever she pleased. And this dress pleased her. It was the kind of dress she'd always secretly longed to wear.

And Amadeo's reaction to it only added to the secret pleasure. To witness his reaction only added to the sense of unchaining herself from the strictures of her old life and embracing the path of the new.

'*Dio*, I want you,' he muttered ardently.

She drifted over to him with a smile, drinking in *his* appearance. Elsbeth wasn't the only one who'd discarded their usual rigid attire for the evening. Amadeo's magnificent, supremely masculine physique was wrapped in tight black chinos with a white shirt and blazer…but the shirts he usually wore were business shirts, not silk, not opened far below his throat. His fitted blazer wasn't usually velvet. And he didn't usually wear a leather chain around his neck with a silver ball at the throat. He'd never looked more devilishly sexy.

Putting her hands on his shoulders, she rose to her tiptoes and whispered, 'When we get home, you can have me.'

Eyes glittering, he bared his teeth. She imagined them sinking into her flesh and shivered as a wave of unadulterated lust thrashed through her. So deep was her desire that she would have let him take her there and then if her bell hadn't

chimed and a maid hurried into the room to tell
them Amadeo's siblings were ready and waiting
for them.

Elsbeth couldn't get over how amazing the party
was, and when Amadeo leaned into her to ask
over the pulsing music if she was enjoying herself she had no hesitation in saying, 'It's the best
party I've ever been to.'

He raised a brow at this.

She giggled. 'I was too nervous to appreciate
our pre-wedding party and our wedding reception.'

'What about parties at the palace?' He said this
casually but she caught the spark of loathing that
always flashed in his eyes whenever Dominic or
anything to do with Monte Cleure was mentioned.

'They were awful. I was so conscious of being
on my best behaviour and not putting a foot wrong
that I might as well have been a mute mannequin.
Believe me, I never drank three glasses of champagne in one sitting there!'

Yes, three glasses of champagne and she was
feeling decidedly lightheaded. But in a good way.
She'd eaten enough of the delicious canapés being
passed around—not as many as Clara, who was
devouring them as if she were afraid there was
going to be an imminent world shortage—and
nibbles to soak up much of the alcohol and stop
her passing the point of tipsy into drunk.

Finally ungluing herself from Amadeo's side a short while later to use the bathroom, she again admired this ultra-modern abode, even if it did strike her as having more an art gallery feel to it than a homely one. Still, all the other guests were tremendously impressed, which she supposed was the whole point. Why spend tens of millions knocking walls down and installing white marble everywhere, floor-to-ceiling windows with a tint that adjusted depending on the strength of the sun and remote-controlled skylights if there was no one to admire it?

When she'd finished in the ladies, she was about to head back to Amadeo when Clara pounced, Alessia at her heels. 'Come with me,' she demanded.

Allowing herself to be dragged out onto the balcony, she quickly realised Alessia was as bemused as she was.

'I can't tell you, so you're going to have to guess,' Clara said the second she'd closed the sliding door behind them. She had possibly the widest smile on her face that Elsbeth had ever seen.

Alessia looked her up and down. A smile formed. 'You're pregnant?'

'Yes! Well guessed!'

Elsbeth looked at Clara's belly, unsure if she'd translated correctly.

Clara nodded, beaming.

Alessia, visibly pregnant herself, threw her

arms around her. After they'd embraced, Clara opened her arms to Elsbeth.

Touched to be included in such a special moment—she wouldn't have blamed her for telling Alessia privately before her—she hugged her tightly, delighted that the woman who was fast becoming a friend was expecting a child.

'Sorry, I've been bursting to tell you,' Clara said when all the hugs and congratulations were done with. 'I've known for a week but Marcelo wanted us to keep it private a bit longer. I wasn't sure if he meant private from the public or private from you too, so I didn't ask him and that way he couldn't confirm it! I've been *itching* for one of you to ask me!'

At that moment the glass door slid open and the man in question appeared. He took one look at the three of them and shook his head indulgently at his wife. 'I knew you'd tell them.'

The mischief on Clara's face made both Elsbeth and Alessia laugh. 'But I'm excited!'

'I've noticed.' But the grin on his own handsome face told Elsbeth that the expectant father was every bit as excited as the expectant mother. 'I suppose I have to tell Amadeo now.'

'And Gabriel,' Alessia piped up, then dashed back into the thrumming party to seek them out and drag them onto the balcony so the good news could be shared with them too.

Much back-slapping and manly hugs ensued,

another bottle of champagne was opened, toasts were raised, crystal tapped against crystal before Clara and Alessia handed their flutes to their husbands to drink for them, and then they headed back inside. Before Elsbeth could rejoin the throng, strong fingers wrapped around her hand and pulled her to a stop.

Thrilling at the heat of his skin against hers, all the more acute as their flesh hadn't made contact since they'd got out of the car, she gazed up into Amadeo's handsome face.

'Are you okay?' he asked, his eyes searching hers.

Understanding his question, recognising the signs of his concern, her heart swelled. Smiling, she nodded and said truthfully, 'I'm thrilled for them.'

'It will happen for us one day.'

'I know.'

The concern turned into the gleam of a smile. Pressing his cheek against hers, he murmured huskily, 'Maybe we should look at making a minor alteration to the rules and adding Wednesdays to our conjugal nights.'

A thrill of joy and wantonness took hold of her and, without even thinking about what she was doing, she clasped hold of his hip and then slid her hand around to clasp a tight buttock. 'I could agree to that.'

Amadeo pulled his head back so he could look

at her flushed face again. 'Just to help the conception process.' And the breaking of the fever. If he couldn't take her away for a week to screw this fever out of them, then he would amend the rules.

'Of course.'

'Original rules applying after conception.' By the time she conceived, the fever would be spent. It was not possible it could continue like this much longer.

Pupils dilated, her fingers squeezed tightly into his buttock. 'Naturally.'

Now he was the one to grab her bottom, pulling her to him and grinding his groin into her. Baring his teeth, he growled, 'Just you wait until I get you home.'

The next hour that passed was, for Amadeo, torture. He'd been so good up to that point on the balcony, ensuring no skin on skin contact with Elsbeth, keeping her by his side but not letting their flesh touch. Now, it was all he could do to keep his loins behaving. The way he was feeling, he was going to have to pour liquid ice down the front of his trousers.

He could hardly believe he'd behaved in such a debauched manner, grinding himself into her like that. Never before had he behaved like that outside the privacy of his own home. When he left the castle's gates, he never forgot who he was, not even in a private setting such as this amongst good friends.

Now it was all he could do not to check his watch every five seconds to see if it was a reasonable time to whisk his wife home.

A large group had formed around them, conversation flowing as freely as the champagne, but the moment it turned eleven he caught Elsbeth's eye. He didn't say anything, just indicated the door.

A knowing sparkle came into her eyes and she gave the subtlest of nods.

Fifteen minutes was all it took to escape the party and then finally they were in the underground garage with their bodyguards, his driver, parked next to Amadeo's siblings' cars and the vehicles used by their individual security details, already opening the back door for them.

Only ten paces away, Elsbeth tugged at his hand and whispered, 'Do our bodyguards *have* to sit in the back with us?'

The fever in his blood was alive in her eyes.

His vocal cords suddenly too thick to reply, he shook his head, then cleared his throat and told his head protection officer to sit up front with the driver. The other guards could arrange themselves in the convoy that always accompanied them.

Enclosed in the back of the car, the only sound was the heaviness of their individual breaths. Elsbeth stared straight ahead, her hands folded neatly on her lap, the rise and fall of her chest rapid.

He couldn't just sense her desire. He could see it. He could *smell* it.

The driver set off.

'Is this cab soundproofed?' she asked huskily.

'Yes. It is completely private...' His assurances had barely left his mouth when she pounced.

In seconds she was straddling his lap, hands clutching his cheeks, her hot mouth devouring him.

Amadeo had long reached an age where he believed nothing could surprise him any more, but the unleashing of Elsbeth's passion took his breath away and the arousal he'd striven to keep abated since their moment on the balcony roared into life.

'I want you inside me,' she muttered before plunging her tongue back into his mouth and scraping her fingers down his chest to the button of his chinos.

And, just like that, the need to be inside her was all-consuming. Thrills like he'd never known in his life ravaged him, Elsbeth's greedy hunger for him feeding his hunger for her. Dragging the lace of her dress to her hips, he grabbed at her lace knickers while she worked on his chinos and, using all his strength, ripped it.

Her mouth still feeding on his, she finally freed the button and unzipped him.

Certain he would combust if he didn't get inside her, Amadeo raised his hips and helped her tug his chinos and boxers low enough to free his raging erection.

There wasn't a moment of hesitation. She sank down on his length, taking him in his entirety in one long motion.

She threw her head back to look at him.

Dio, it felt as if he was seeing her for the first time. The cloak had gone. This was Elsbeth in all her uninhibited beauty. She was shaking with desire.

And so was he.

Cheeks flushed, pulsing eyes dark and heavy-lidded, she rested her hands on his shoulders and began to ride him.

Mio dio… This was incredible.

She was incredible. Exquisite.

Grabbing the bodice of her dress, he yanked it down to expose her naked breasts. Immediately, he took one in his mouth. Immediately, she clasped the back of his head to keep him there. Her moans deepened, her movements increasing in tempo until her head was thrashing, her nails digging into his skull and she was grinding down on him, crying out his name, the thickening force of her climax pulling him into his own exultant release.

Elsbeth, her cheek pressed tightly against Amadeo's, did nothing to stop the bubble of laughter from escaping.

For the first time in her life she'd let herself lose control and it had been unbelievable. Shy Elsbeth Fernandez would never have believed that hidden in her frightened heart had been a wanton, sensual woman capable of and, more importantly, willing to follow her basest desires.

She hadn't planned it. Not in the slightest. She couldn't have done it if she'd planned it! It had been hard keeping her composure after their scene on the balcony but she'd managed it, managed the heat simmering beneath her skin and the tingles of awareness that danced on it to act the part of gracious guest. Then they'd left the party together and that awareness had accelerated, knowing they were on the verge of being alone together and all the glorious things they would do…and in an instant the hot spot between her legs had become a pulsating mass of need.

What had followed…

She pressed herself even tighter against him, the man who had brought her out of her shy shell, the man who'd encouraged the dropping of the protective mask she wore, the man who'd encouraged her to be *her*.

Without Amadeo, the wanton, sensual woman would still be hiding in her frightened heart.

Another bubble of laughter rose up her throat. She wasn't frightened any more!

He moved his face to kiss her. 'You're incredible,' he breathed.

She sighed with a dreamy smile and gazed into his clear green eyes. 'I love you.'

CHAPTER THIRTEEN

As SOON AS the words escaped Elsbeth's lips they both froze. The shock in Amadeo's eyes mirrored the cold shock in her chest.

Where on earth had that come from?

Nowhere.

Recovering herself, she laughed. 'Well, that was one slip of the tongue—I meant that I love *sex* with you.'

That was the absolute truth, even if she hadn't actually meant to say anything at all. Amadeo had drawn out the woman in her and taught her not only of the joy in uninhibited, mutually fulfilling sex but that there was nothing shameful in embracing pleasure.

It wasn't possible she had meant more than that. It had been the heat of the moment, all those feelings fizzing through her—*still* fizzing through her—that had made her tongue run away with itself.

A beat passed; a tiny moment in time that seemed to stretch to the moon and back before Amadeo laughed too and kissed her. 'Sexy woman,' he growled, then kissed her again.

Relief that she'd covered her unwitting faux pas and hadn't caused any damage blew out the cold shock.

Uncoupling themselves, they straightened their clothing and held hands until they arrived back at the castle.

I love you.

Amadeo closed his eyes to the accounts printed off in preparation for his quarterly meeting with the team who ran the Berrutis' vast art collection, and kneaded his temples.

I love you.

His heart had come to an abrupt halt at those dreamily delivered words three nights ago. His lungs had closed. Time had hung suspended.

And then Elsbeth had laughed and made her quip about loving sex with him, and then he'd laughed and the moment had passed as if it had never been said.

The more time that had passed since then though, the louder those three words echoed in his ears. He'd spent their engagements the day before surreptitiously observing her, looking for any changes in behaviour or demeanour, but she was the same as she always was, gently wry, softly cool, calmly collected.

He wished he could say the same for himself. It

felt like he had something acrid living in his guts, churning and coiling.

She *couldn't* have meant it. That was what he kept telling himself. It was a misfiring of words as she'd so quickly explained. She'd been as shocked at them as he had. No, she definitely hadn't meant it. Elsbeth was no fool. She knew their marriage would never be like the marriages of his siblings and had never even hinted at deviating from the rules laid out before they'd exchanged their vows.

James, his private secretary, who'd he'd poached from the British royal family with the lure of Ceres' fantastic climate, entered his office. What he said pulled Amadeo sharply out of his thoughts.

'Dominic wants me to do *what*?' he asked, astounded.

'Have an informal race once the Grand Prix's finished,' James repeated. 'It's his understanding that one of the racing teams has agreed to lend their cars to you for the event.'

As tempting a proposition as it was to get behind the wheel of a racing car and publicly thrash the monster, there was no way he could accept. James knew that perfectly well.

'I assume you've already declined for me?'

'Yes, Your Highness, but as the request came from a monarch, I thought it best to inform you of it in case it came up in conversation between you.'

The thought of even talking to Dominic Fernandez made his already roiling guts churn harder.

He knew why King Pig—it was astounding how quickly Clara's nickname for him had stuck in his head; he'd have to be careful not to utter it publicly—wanted to race him. King Pig, for all his ego, was an insecure monster. Thick-skinned enough to try and force a woman who viscerally hated him into marriage, he was also thick-skinned enough to think he could cultivate a close relationship with his cousin's husband. And that was because King Pig, for all his thick skin, was also an insecure toad who craved acceptance by his peers. Turning Monte Cleure into a billionaires' tax haven and basking in the caviar-stuffed fools' so-called friendship wasn't enough for him. He wanted to bask in the approval and acceptance of his fellow royals. It must drive him insane that Europe's royal families disdained him, only inviting him to the events that protocol dictated they should.

King Pig had assumed Amadeo's marriage to his cousin would mean closer ties between the two men. King Pig was likely smarting that Amadeo and the rest of the Berrutis had maintained the distance they'd always kept between them. King Pig likely knew of Amadeo's financial involvement in Sébastien's team and his great interest in the sport. King Pig likely assumed a race between the two men would forge a bond between them.

King Pig also likely assumed that the experience he had behind a racing wheel—his crash notwithstanding—meant he would easily beat the heir to the Ceres throne and thus earn himself the kudos money and status just could not buy.

King Pig was too thick-skinned to get it into his thick head that Amadeo would sooner spit on the man than play his games, even if he wasn't in a position to accept the offer of a race.

'Anything else?' he asked, noticing that James was still hovering.

'Princess Elsbeth came to your offices.'

Just the mention of her name made his heart judder and a coldness seep through his veins, and in that instant it came to him why those three little unwittingly delivered words were plaguing him: Elsbeth *never* spoke without thinking. She never made a slip of the tongue, and that she'd made this one straight after the height of passion...

He forced himself to concentrate on the rest of what James had to say.

'She asked you to call her if you have free time before your meeting, but said that it's not important.'

Amadeo inhaled sharply and nodded. 'Thank you.'

Once alone again, he rubbed his pounding forehead.

This couldn't continue. If he wasn't careful, he was going to waste the time needed to prepare for his imminent meeting thinking about Elsbeth. He'd wasted enough time as it was.

This was the kind of behaviour he'd been infuriated at his brother for displaying, the lapses of concentration when he'd known damn well Marcelo was thinking about Clara instead of the important work at hand.

It was the kind of behaviour he'd never been susceptible to before and he wasn't going to start now.

He forced his entire focus onto the pages before him.

Elsbeth could wait.

Late afternoon and Elsbeth stood at the edge of the garden watching as a team of landscapers, supervised by head gardener Pep, excavated sections of the lawn to the design she and Pep had agreed between them. This was the manual part of the landscaping project that she couldn't be physically involved in, but it brought her joy to watch the slow transformation, and she took frequent photos on the professional camera she'd bought for herself to document it.

She sensed Amadeo's approach before he stood beside her, and turned her face to smile at him. 'Good day?'

'Long day. I'm sorry, I didn't get a chance to call you back.'

She shrugged. 'That's okay. I knew you were

busy. I was just going to see if I could tempt you into sharing lunch with me before your meeting started.'

'Sorry. Another time.'

'I'll hold you to that,' she said softly.

The pause that followed passed just a fraction too long before he nodded at the landscape team. 'Looks like they're making good progress. Are you pleased with what they've done so far?'

'Very much, although I think they're less pleased that I've spent most of the day openly spying on them. They'll be glad I'll be out of their hair tomorrow.' They had a full day of engagements scheduled.

He gave a quick smile. 'Let us hope the presence of a beautiful princess isn't too distracting for them.'

'They do seem very keen to work without tops on,' she mused. 'But as they haven't yet invited me to take my own top off, I'm sure they're managing the distraction just fine.'

His next smile was fractionally warmer and almost met his eyes. Then he looked at his watch. 'I need to go back in. Oh, and before I forget, I'm going to have to cancel our plans for tomorrow night—I need to do an overnight in Milan. There's a couple of issues the art team have brought to my attention that need to be resolved in person. I'll fly there straight from our last engagement and return Friday morning.'

Elsbeth, determined to keep her composure, arranged her face before saying, 'Am I not invited too?' Now that the frequency of their engagements had lessened, their schedule until the end of the year consisted of the majority being condensed into two days a week. Her diary for the next day was empty.

He shook his head and grimaced. 'It's purely work. You'd be bored...' a glimmer suddenly flashed in his eyes '...*and* a distraction.' He looked at his watch again. 'I really do need to go. My mother's expecting me. Enjoy your spying.'

Elsbeth waited until he'd disappeared from view, then sedately made her way back into her quarters.

Alone, she sat on her new red armchair and breathed in slowly ten times.

After they'd laughed off her 'I love you', they'd returned to the castle, where Amadeo had promptly made love to her in the shower and stayed until the sun had come up. When he'd left, it had been with the promise of dinner in his quarters on that Wednesday evening, a promise that had *thrilled* her. Increasing the times they were together privately *and* being admitted into her husband's private sanctuary after all this time and making love in his bed...?

Slowly but surely, the rules he'd laid down on their wedding night, those said and those unsaid, were being dismantled. For the first time she'd allowed herself to dream of a future where they lived together as husband and wife, not separately as two individuals who just happened to be married and were trying to make a baby together. It was a dream that made her heart sing and her veins fizz, and made her confront a truth—that though her unbidden declaration of love had been a slip of the tongue, she could no longer deny that it contained more than a grain of truth. She was falling for him.

It was a truth she wished had kept itself hidden.

Her first real inkling that something was wrong had come yesterday during their engagements. They never showed any affection in work time. They didn't touch each other. That was normal. Amadeo was heir to the throne and she would be his queen consort. Standards needed to be maintained and that meant a dignified front befitting their status.

It was his eyes that had changed. The way he looked at her. She'd caught a few hungry looks from him but there had been no stripping her naked with his stare. The only thing it had felt like he was trying to strip was her skull so he could bore into her head. Conversation between them had been as easy as it had grown to be in recent weeks but there had been no hint of intimacy in his tone. Just little things that had made her feel that something was off and that he was pulling away from her, but small enough to make her uncertain whether or not she was being paranoid.

And now he'd cancelled their date.

But he'd looked stressed, she argued with herself. Maybe those issues identified with the art collection were more serious than she'd supposed. As the Berrutis did not accept a single cent from the public purse, amongst many other sources of income they monetised their highly prized art collection. Amadeo had taken control of the billion-euro collection on the family's behalf when he turned twenty-one, and it was a lot of work, even with a team running it on his behalf.

Or, even better, maybe he was stressed because he had to cancel their date. After all, he *had* called her a distraction. And promised they would do it another time.

Having successfully cheered herself up, she pulled her phone out of her pocket, called Clara and arranged to spend Thursday at a master sculptor's workshop as inspiration for her garden... And as a distraction to stop herself mooning and talking herself into making mountains out of molehills.

Late Saturday night, Amadeo lay on his back, Elsbeth using his chest like a pillow, her leg hooked around his thigh, an arm draped across his stomach. Her fingers were making idle circular sweeping motions over his skin.

'Who would you be married to, if you were born into a different family and hadn't married me to escape Dominic?' he asked into the peaceful silence.

Only the silence was peaceful. A week ago, Elsbeth had told him she loved him. The churning in his guts had got even stronger as the week had gone on. Knots had formed too, little tendrils in his chest knitting together and slowly tightening.

She tilted her head to look at him. 'I don't know. Why do you ask?'

'It's a question you once asked me.'

'Yes, but you never answered.'

'You answer me and I'll answer you.'

'You told me a woman shouldn't ask about a man's fantasies unless she was prepared for the answer. Or something like that.'

'That was then.' And this was now. Love had been mentioned when she should have known it was a forbidden word. She couldn't love him. She mustn't love him. He didn't want her heart. He'd never wanted it.

Lust was the most he could give Elsbeth. Lust would burn itself out and, when it did, Elsbeth would be his princess and then, one day, his queen consort. Together they would be the figureheads of his great nation, dignified assets his countrymen could look up to with pride, leading his family and the children he hoped to have by example. Messy emotions such as love, the kind his siblings enjoyed, were just that. Messy. They infected thinking. They turned perfectly reasonable people into hormonal adolescent-like creatures.

Just look at his sister. He couldn't use Marcelo as an example as he'd always had problems with his impulse control, but Alessia had never been afflicted, not until she'd stupidly let her hormones get the better of her and had an unprotected one-night stand. His dutiful sister hadn't been the same since, falling in love with her husband and often prioritising him and their growing child over her duties, recently announcing that from now on she'd only be undertaking one weekend evening engagement a month. He couldn't even begrudge her for it, though he wanted to. Love and emotions became so deeply entangled in people that their priorities changed and clear thinking went out of the window. It was beyond the realms of credulity that Amadeo would ever succumb to such nonsense. Elsbeth should know that.

It had been lust, and only lust, that had driven him to tweak the rules of his marriage, tweaks he now strongly suspected had made Elsbeth believe would lead to further tweaks until, bit by bit, everything agreed was dismantled and they became the couple they could never be.

He hoped his suspicions were wrong and that he was putting thoughts in her head that weren't there but, right or wrong, he needed to take them a step back and disabuse her of this thinking. He didn't really think she was in love with him…did he?…but, whether she was or wasn't, he didn't want to hurt her. Not his sweet Elsbeth. She'd suffered enough hurt in her life. Better lead her away from thoughts of a romantic love subtly and then, by the time their fever was finally spent, she would be as content as him to live separate lives as originally agreed, and everything would work out perfectly for both of them.

'Go on, tell me,' he coaxed. 'Given free choice, what kind of man would you have married? Who would have been your ideal husband?'

Dragging herself so her breasts were crushed against his chest and she could look at him properly, she said, 'I never had a specific fantasy man in my head. My dreams were always of an English cottage with a colourful, rambling garden and someone kind to live in it with me.'

For some reason, this answer made his sharp, knotted chest tighten into a point. 'You would have had to learn the language to live in England,' he pointed out, running his fingers up and down the soft skin of her back.

'I'd have used the translation app Clara made me download.'

'I'm sure your faceless husband would have helped you learn.'

She brushed her thumb over his mouth and smiled. 'He might not have had your patience.'

'Your improvement in my language has nothing to do with me.'

'Of course it does. You always translate for me when I need it, and you get people to speak slowly to make it easier for me to understand.'

'A husband who married you for love would have helped you far more, but that is the nature of ordinary people's marriages; they become couples in a way you and I can never be. But I don't suppose it is worth comparing the marriage we have with the ones we could have had if we'd been free to choose. All we had were pipe dreams we both knew could never come true. Take me, if I'd had free choice, if I'd been born plain Amadeo and not Prince Amadeo, I would have been a racing driver.'

Elsbeth's heart thudded heavily, the euphoria of their lovemaking dissolving. She didn't know if she was making another mountain out of a molehill but this all sounded like a veiled warning to her sensitive ears. If she was prone to paranoia, she could believe Amadeo had started the whole conversation just to compare their marriage to a marriage built on love.

She hesitated before asking, 'And your wife? Who would she be?'

'I've never had a particular physical type but, given the choice, I would have chosen someone fun and outgoing with a zest for life, but I don't know if that's in response to the discreet women

I've always been obliged to date, the allure of forbidden fruit. An ordinary man isn't bound to discretion like a prince. But then, I don't think I would have married at all had I been an ordinary man. I've never been susceptible to the kinds of emotion that leads an ordinary man into committing his life to someone.'

'Fun and outgoing.' Three words that pierced like an icy knife in Elsbeth's chest. As casually as Amadeo had explained it, they sounded pointed to her, a reiteration of the time he'd baldly stated he would never have chosen her for his wife. No one had ever used 'fun and outgoing' to describe Elsbeth. Shy and sweet were the usual descriptors.

And as for him not being susceptible to emotions like an ordinary man… How could that be interpreted as anything but a warning?

Before she could make proper sense of any of this, he rolled her onto her back and gazed into her eyes with that hooded, lascivious stare that always made her pelvis melt.

'Whoever I would or would not have married given a choice, I guarantee that woman wouldn't be as sexy as you.' And then his mouth closed on hers, and all her thoughts and fears dissolved under the heat consuming her.

Elsbeth's sense of paranoia grew the next Wednesday when Amadeo joined her in her quarters. They shared a meal. They spent the night making love. He was as worshipful of her body and as adventurous a lover as the one she'd come to adore. They slept wrapped in each other's arms. He left when the sun rose.

But there had been something missing. It was in the way he'd held her after making love. A subtle mental detachment, as if his mind was far away from her. She sensed it was deliberate.

There had been no more talk of her being invited into his quarters.

Another week passed, Groundhog Week repeated. Engagements. Supervision of the garden. Saturday and Wednesday night: fantastic sex with her husband. And then the following weekend arrived.

Instead of dining with her on the Friday night like she'd become accustomed to him doing, Amadeo announced he was going for a night out with his friend Sébastien, who was on the island for a flying visit before that weekend's race in Belgium. There had been no suggestion that Elsbeth join them.

By the time Amadeo finally joined her on Saturday morning, nausea had settled so heavily in her stomach that even him pouncing on her the moment he walked in the door had hardly soothed it.

Later that night, long after he'd fallen asleep, she forced herself to look the facts in the face.

His words about ordinary marriages and emotions *had* been a warning.

All progress between them had stopped.

They were going backwards.

He was pulling away from her, and there was no point in burying her head in the sand about it any longer.

While they took each other to the heights of pleasure—she had no inhibitions with him at all now—a growing humiliation burned that she was essentially a slave for the touch of a man who only wanted her in the bedroom. She had to face the facts Amadeo had practically spelled out to her that, as far as he was concerned, they would never have a real marriage. Their lives would always be separate, and he wasn't going to include her in his any more than was necessary.

It was no coincidence that he'd spelled it out to her a week after she'd slipped up and told him she loved him and only days after his last-minute trip to Milan that she'd been deliberately excluded from.

He shifted in his sleep, throwing his leg over hers, the top of his dark head nudging against hers, and she squeezed her eyes shut as a wave of painful affection surged through her. Rolling onto her side, she wrapped her arms around him and held him tightly, trying to think of the situation in a more positive light. Was their marriage not a million times better than she'd dared hope when she'd first arrived in this country? Were they not perfectly matched in the bedroom? Did she not instigate their lovemaking as much as he did?

But these positive thoughts lasted less time than a climax. Because the painful gape that always used to form around her shrivelling heart after a climax had returned, and now it was a wound that ached unbearably.

It was the agonising ache that came from falling head over heels in love with a man who could never return that love.

She screwed up her eyes even tighter, trying desperately to stop the hot tears from leaking. She mustn't cry, not when the tears would fall onto him.

When she finally had her emotions under control, she relaxed her hold and opened her eyes. The room was lightening. The sun was rising. Soon, Amadeo would wake and leave her to spend his Sunday without her...

Elsbeth's heart made a sudden leap.

Sunday?

It was Sunday?

Placing a hand to her pounding chest, she quickly told herself not to get her hopes up. Just because her period was as regular as clockwork and for the first time in a decade hadn't started on a Saturday didn't have to mean anything.

CHAPTER FOURTEEN

WHEN AMADEO WAS admitted into Elsbeth's quarters that Wednesday evening, the anticipation was every bit as strong as always, its strength a relief that he hadn't thought of a way to get out of seeing her for an extra evening each week.

Dragging himself out of her bed got harder each time but the demons that had plagued him after her declaration of love were now well under control and he felt lighter in himself than he had in a long time. This fever for his wife would break soon. He'd already proved it, imposing himself on Sébastien on Friday night just to assure himself that he wasn't addicted to his scheduled time with her. It had been a fantastic night, with excellent food, the best wine and talk that was all things motor sport. He didn't deny that Elsbeth had accompanied him to Sébastien's in her own way, a spectre in the corner of his eye that floated into his vision whenever he wasn't actively thinking of her, but that didn't prove his addiction to her. When the fever broke, she would stop haunting his dreams as well as filling his thoughts. Everything would be as it should.

She was waiting for him in her day room. By now, there were so many changes to the furniture and furnishings that it was hardly the same room that had been created for her. The changes made it as warm and bright as the woman who'd chosen them. They suited her. They would suit him too...

Where the actual hell had that thought come from?

One look at her and the random thought, along with his intention of carrying her off to bed before their dinner was served, was forgotten. She was as pale as he'd ever seen her, her usually bright eyes sunken.

She hesitated before rising from her armchair.

He strode over so he could look more closely at her. 'Are you not feeling well?' She'd been looking a bit peaky these last few days but he'd assumed that was her period which, even with the medication, was never easy for her.

'I've not been sleeping well.'

Alarmed, he reached for his phone. 'I'll call Dr Jessop...'

She put a hand on his arm. 'I've already seen him.'

'When?'

'After our morning engagement. I'm pregnant.'

His brain froze. His mouth opened. Nothing came out.

A small smile formed on her lips. 'Why don't you sit down?'

Unable to tear his gaze from her, he absently ran his fingers through his hair. 'You're pregnant?'

The small smile still there, she nodded. 'Dr Jessop brought a test with him and confirmed it.'

Realisation began to dawn. They were going to have a baby. He was going to be a father. Elsbeth was going to be a mother.

A spasm of pure, unadulterated joy shot through him and he pulled her to him, wrapping his arms tightly around her, breathing in Elsbeth's wonderful perfume and the honey scent of her shampoo. Until that moment, he hadn't realised how deep his own longing for a child was. 'That is just the best news you could have given me.' Pulling back a little so he could plant an enormous kiss to her mouth, he then cupped her cheeks and rained more kisses over every millimetre of her face.

'Why didn't you tell me your period was late?' he asked when he'd finished kissing her and wrapped his arms back around her.

'We haven't been alone for me to tell you.'

'You could have said you had something to tell me in private or come to my quarters.'

'I'm not allowed in your quarters and, in any case, I was trying not to build my hopes up.'

'What do you mean, you're not *allowed* in my quarters? Of course you're allowed.'

'I've never been invited into them. Can you let me go now, please? I can't breathe.'

He loosened his hold and swung her into his arms. 'Let's go to bed and celebrate.' A nice gentle bout of lovemaking would put some colour back in her cheeks.

But instead of throwing her arms around his neck and devouring his mouth like she normally did when he carried her, she wriggled against him. 'Please put me down.'

Immediately concerned, he placed her on the nearest sofa and sat himself beside her. 'Are you feeling unwell? Are you suffering from sickness? Is it the pregnancy causing it?'

How Elsbeth wished he wasn't displaying such solicitousness. She'd known he'd be pleased about the pregnancy but hadn't imagined he'd be this delighted. It only made what she needed to say harder.

Straightening, she tugged her hand out of his then linked her fingers together and rested them on her lap. 'No, I'm not ill and it's too soon for pregnancy sickness.'

'Then what is it?'

She took a deep breath and arranged her face. 'We agreed on our wedding night that once a baby was conceived, we would no longer share a bed.'

The way his handsome head reared back and his mouth opened and closed was almost comical. She assumed his excitement about the pregnancy had made him temporarily forget about the rules. It made her glad that she was the one to remind him and enforce them. She didn't think she'd be able to keep her composure if he'd been the one to say the closeness they'd found had to be severed with immediate effect. It would have come after he'd taken her to bed again. After he'd sated his lust.

At least this way she got to salvage a little of her dignity. Amadeo didn't want a real marriage with her. His heart was frozen to her. He would never love her.

She doubted he could love anyone.

He bowed his head, his composure regained, and then locked his eyes on hers. 'We both know we're not ready to stop being intimate with each other.'

'I am.'

'You're what?'

'Ready.'

Amadeo leaned in closer, eyes narrowing as they bored deep into hers, searching, searching. 'You're lying.'

'No.' One syllable, delivered so curtly it would be believable if her plump lips and chin weren't trembling.

He dropped his voice into a caress. 'You expect me to believe the desire you feel for me has ended overnight?'

She lifted her trembling chin with a hint of defiancé. 'I didn't say that. I said I was ready to stop acting on it, as per the rules we agreed on our wedding night. Rules *you* imposed.'

Ah. *Now* he understood where this was coming from. Elsbeth was afraid he was going to enforce the rules himself and end the intimacy between them. If she only knew how hard he'd already tried to wean himself off her, her fears would evaporate.

He palmed her cheek, marvelling as he always did at how soft it felt against his skin. He inched his face closer still and whispered, 'Rules that can be tweaked if we are both in agreement.'

They'd tweaked the rules already, to their mutual satisfaction. Why not carry on as they were when things were so good between them?

'But I'm not in agreement.' Oh, God, Elsbeth hadn't meant to sound so tremulous but it was so hard holding onto her resolve when her body thrummed so madly from being held in his arms. And Amadeo heard it too. She saw it in the way his eyes gleamed.

His lips brushed against hers. The hand caressing her cheek gently drifted down her neck. She shivered at the tingles it set off.

'You are really willing to give up such pleasure?' he murmured sensually. 'To never feel our naked skin as one again...'

Lower his fingers dragged, over the swell of her breast, his thumb encircling her puckered nipple, sending a strong bolt of need straight into her pelvis.

Stop it, she begged with her eyes. *Don't do this to me. This needs to end now.*

'To never feel my tongue where you like it the most…'

His fingers drifted down and over her abdomen. His breaths, hot against her mouth, were getting heavier. Elsbeth's breaths were getting heavier too. The sensations he was evoking…

His fingers tiptoed to the band of her skirt. God help her, she was trembling with desire. 'To never ride me the way that makes you lose yourself so…'

A finger slid beneath the band and pressed into the skin of her belly. The shock of electricity from his touch was strong enough to bring her to her senses by injecting a huge dose of humiliated rage to the fire in her veins.

Grabbing his hand, she shoved it away from her with a, 'Get *off*,' and clumsily jumped to her feet.

For the second time in as many minutes, he looked as if she'd punched him.

'How *dare* you try to seduce me when I've just told you I don't want your seduction any more?' she cried. 'Which part of *I'm not in agreement* did you think you could just ignore?'

Amadeo stood, palms raised, staring at her like a zoo keeper whose placid charge has just turned rabid. He'd wanted to see colour back in her cheeks but not this angry stain.

'This isn't you talking, Elsbeth,' he said steadily.
'This is the hormones from the pregnancy.' Hadn't
he seen how pregnancy hormones affected his sister in the early stages, making her cry easily when
she'd so rarely cried before?

'Don't you patronise me!' she snapped. 'The
only thing the pregnancy has to do with my decision is that it's forced me to think clearly. I'm your
wife but I'm not your partner, and you've made
it perfectly obvious that what we have now is as
far as you're prepared to go. You've reached your
limit and now I've reached *my* limit. I'd rather
spend the rest of my life celibate than share a bed
with a man who only wants me to slake his lust.
You're the one who made me see that I'm not on
this earth to be a vessel for your pleasure and that
I have the freedom to live my life within these
castle walls however I choose. Well, I've made
that choice and I choose to live it without you.'

Her words sliced through him, landing in his
chest with icy, jagged barbs. 'I have never treated
you like a *vessel*.'

'That's exactly how you've treated me. It's how
you've treated me from the moment we married. I
could have been anyone lying there beneath you.'

'You can't tell me you didn't get pleasure and
satisfaction from it,' he retorted, breathing heavily.

'Physical pleasure but no emotional pleasure.
No affection. Nothing to make me feel you saw

me as a human being with feelings. And I notice you don't deny it.'

'What is there to deny? I've never hidden that I married you for the sake of my nation and the monarchy. I did my best to be gentle with you and leave you satisfied and I know damn well I achieved both those things, but you know too how I felt about you back then. How could I fake affection for a woman whose very name left me cold?'

'I was a stranger in a new home and you left me alone!' she cried, her voice rising. 'That wasn't cold, that was cruel, but I was so terrified of being sent back to the man whose name is responsible for your coldness towards me that, even if I had recognised your cruelty for what it was, I would never have spoken out. Not then.'

'I was never intentionally cruel,' he raged, furious at this character assassination. 'I did everything I could to give you a home you would feel happy and comfortable in, and you know damn well too how much more of an effort I made once I was aware of your loneliness. I've given you every support in everything you've done or wanted to do.'

'Give yourself a pat on the back then and tell yourself what a great man you are. And in many ways you *are* a great man and I know it's unfair of me to throw things in your face that are in the past, but they're things that still affect us today. They affect *me*. I know you made an effort with me because I could see it. I know you hated your desire for me because I sensed you fighting it. Things have been so good between us this last month but still I sense you fighting and trying to pull away and dropping hints to push me away. Whether it's because you will never accept the blood in my veins or because you're so used to thinking you're right about everything that you can't admit to yourself that you were wrong about me, or because you really do think yourself so damn superior to human emotion... I don't know! The only thing I *am* sure of is that you've never given us a chance. You will never give us a chance. You've fought your feelings for me every inch of the way and now I'm sick of the fight.'

The vein in his temple was jumping, the only sign of life on features that had turned to granite. Elsbeth refused to let it sway her from what needed to be said.

'Nearly three months we've been married, Amadeo,' she said, 'and I've never slept in your bed. You're never going to let me in and be a real wife to you and you will never let yourself be a real husband to me, and sooner or later I'm going to start hating you for it. I don't want to hate you, especially not when I'm carrying your child, so this ends now. I will not share a bed with you again and unless you want me to assert my freedom and independence even further and move out of the castle altogether, respect my decision and autonomy, just as I have respected every decision you've made, even the ones I didn't like or agree with. As of now, our marriage reverts to our original agreement.'

The cold roar in Amadeo's head was deafening. The slicing of Elsbeth's words had spread, tearing at his throat and shredding his guts, his lungs… but not his heart. No, that particular organ had incrementally hardened at her twisting of everything they'd shared, and solidified into something impenetrable as her threats landed.

The vein in his temple was still jumping madly, his expression one Elsbeth could no longer read. Slowly, his body came back to life. His neck lifted, his nostrils flared as his chest and shoulders rose. He gave a short incline of his head and a terse, 'As you wish.'

And then he turned on his heel and walked out of her quarters for the last time.

Amadeo prepared himself for the next day's engagement in his usual fashion. Shower. Shave. Brush his teeth. Dress himself in the outfit he'd previously selected and which a member of his domestic team had laid out for him. Style his hair. Splash cologne to his cheeks. Head down the stairs to their shared reception area.

Elsbeth appeared moments later.

'Good morning,' she said politely.

'Good morning.'

And then they were whisked out to their waiting car by their teams.

On the drive, the usual chatter, led by his private secretary, filled the cabin of the car, a refresher of the imminent engagement and pertinent points to remember. When they arrived, the usual crowd awaited them. The usual tour was given, the usual speeches and further walkabout made. Then it was back in the car for the return journey.

Their week's engagements now over, James moved talk on to the weekend's Grand Prix, the banquet they were hosting and the King of Monte Cleure's overnight stay at the castle.

It was only when the King's name was mentioned that Amadeo flicked his gaze to Elsbeth. Up to that point he'd successfully tuned her out as Elsbeth, forging her in his mind as his faceless consort for the day. It was best to keep her faceless in his own mind until his fury with her abated, because, of course, he could not let it out. In public and amongst staff, a prince was dignified and regal at all times. He couldn't let it out in private either. In one swift move, Elsbeth had severed their relationship and made it impossible for him to have a voice in the severing. He had no doubt her threat to move out of the castle had been real. If he set foot in her quarters uninvited she would leave. If she left, scandal would ensue.

Where will you go? he longed to spit at her. *You have nothing without me.*

But that wasn't strictly true. She had money. Her own money. A bank account he'd had opened for her so she never felt trapped and helpless as she'd been in her old life.

He'd given her all the tools to live her life as an autonomous woman, given her all the encouragement to embrace her freedom, and look how she repaid him. With threats. Threats that were not empty.

So, to keep his loathing suppressed, he'd imagined her faceless, but the mention of Dominic's name instantly turned her back into flesh and blood, and as her beautiful face came back into focus, with it came a reminder of the torrid, fearful life she'd lived before she came to Ceres.

Before he could drag his stare away, her eyes suddenly darted to his.

One heart-stopping look passed between them, and then she blinked and the mask she'd always worn so well slipped back on.

He hardened his heart.

Amadeo stood on his balcony looking out over the garden. It had changed beyond all recognition. The neat and orderly space had turned into a wonder of shapes and colours, with snaking pathways, a large pond with a bench, a pagoda, quirky artistic statues, fruit trees, giant olive trees, cherry blossoms and an abundance of vividly coloured plants and flowers. And still it wasn't finished. Patches of soil indicated the spaces Elsbeth was still to fill with yet more colour. No doubt she'd be out there that afternoon while Amadeo and a good chunk of his countrymen were at the racetrack for Ceres' most popular Grand Prix.

He'd watched her work at it many times from behind his French doors. Never showing his face. Hiding away. Admiring the care she took over each and every plant. Heart tightening at the contentment on her face.

He concentrated on breathing. Since Elsbeth had severed the personal side of their marriage, there had been a bitter coiling in his guts. Every day that passed, the coil tightened, his body filled with something so malignant that no workout in his gym could even start to expel it from him. The only relief came when he looked out onto her garden.

Would their child inherit her love of gardening? Or his love of fast cars? Two polar opposite pastimes, one designed to soothe, the other to thrill.

Elsbeth did both. To watch her garden, to just be in her presence and listen to her quiet voice was to soothe him. To look at her, to get naked under the sheets with her was to thrill him.

His heart thumped hard against his ribs, almost winding him.

Elsbeth was like the flowers she'd planted. She'd arrived at his castle like an under-watered, wilting wallflower and slowly but surely blossomed into a passionate, colourful, highly scented frangipani.

Another even harder thump slammed into him and he bent over, gasping.

Why hadn't he defended himself? Her words had enraged him but he'd done little to stop them and nothing at the end to try and change her mind. He'd walked away from her without defending himself, without fighting for her. And why? Because nearly everything she'd said was true.

The only thing she'd been wrong about was her blood. He'd long ago stopped looking at her as anything but Elsbeth. His wife.

Everything else…

He *had* seduced her for his own pleasure. He'd revelled in the unravelling of her sexuality because he was the lucky recipient of it. He'd done all that while pushing her back and back every time she got too close, clinging stubbornly to those damned rules, believing himself immune to human emotion—no, call it true as Elsbeth had done: believing himself *superior* to it.

The agony suffocating him meant he could deny it no more.

He wasn't superior to or immune to emotion.

The woman whose defences he'd been so intent on breaking down had silently seeped under the defences of his own skin and embedded herself into his heart.

CHAPTER FIFTEEN

'HOW ARE YOU finding marriage to my cousin?' King Pig asked, having just squeezed his obese body to the front of the barrier to stand beside Amadeo. Loath though Amadeo had been to offer Dominic a seat in the royal enclosure of the Ceres National Racetrack, protocol—and his mother—demanded it. He'd filled the enclosure with dignitaries and trustees of a number of the charities he patronised, partly in the hope of diluting his presence, but Dominic had stuck close to him like a bad smell until Amadeo had excused himself on a made-up pretext. Now he'd been hunted down again.

He gripped the top of the barrier. The race was almost over. Only two more laps. 'Very well,' he lied.

'She is a good wife to you?'

'Yes.'

King Pig leaned in closer and dropped his voice. 'My sources tell me she's pregnant.'

Gritting his teeth both at the question and the

foulness of Dominic's breath, Amadeo gave a tight nod and received a hearty slap on the back.

'My congratulations. A new Berruti heir. You must be relieved your virility has proved itself. You are hoping for a boy?'

Glad he was wearing shades against the autumn sun, Amadeo kept his tone neutral. 'A healthy child is all I hope for.'

'Sure, sure.' He dropped his voice again. 'That's what we all have to say in this age of equality, eh? I take it the pregnancy means my cousin is to your liking.' His eyebrows waggled leeringly.

'Elsbeth is a credit to your nation.'

'She is a real lady, the jewel of my nation.' He waggled his eyebrows again, his expression somehow managing to become even more lecherous. 'There's something about virgins, isn't there? You can break them in and mould them into what you want them to be.' He leaned in even closer, his mouth practically touching Amadeo's ear to whisper, 'When the baby comes and she can't service you any more, let me know. I can arrange another virgin to warm your bed.'

Something inside him snapped. The malignant, bitter coil suddenly unleashed in a ricochet of disgust and loathing. Turning abruptly to face him, Amadeo looked Dominic up and down with a sneer. 'I've changed my mind. I will race you. Three laps.'

Dominic's piggy eyes gleamed. 'Ah, so you *are* man enough.'

Now Amadeo was the one to lean into the shorter man and savagely whisper, 'Man enough not to abuse virgins for my own pleasure, you sick bastard.'

Even though Dominic's face turned puce, it didn't give even a modicum of satisfaction.

'Three laps. I will see you on the start line in one hour…that's if you can fit in the seat. I'll make sure they have a vat of grease to help you in.'

The first driver crossed the finish line and the crowd erupted, shouts and cheers ringing so loudly that any retort Dominic might have found would have been drowned out.

Leaving him gawping like an outraged goldfish, Amadeo turned his back on King Pig and, his bodyguards making the heaving crowd part for him, found his father and informed him that he would be making the trophy presentation instead. Not explaining himself, he left the enclosure to find Sébastien and demanded the use of his test car. He wouldn't be able to refuse, not when Amadeo owned sixty percent of the team.

He would race Dominic. Race him, beat him and humiliate him. And then he would put all his energy, and all his money if necessary, into bringing this vile monster down.

Elsbeth was planting climbing roses in the garden when Clara came flying out through her patio door, shouting her name.

Abandoning her plants, she hurried over to her. 'What's wrong?'

But the run Clara had made from her quarters to Elsbeth's had winded her and she bent over, gasping, 'Amadeo.'

A prickle of ice nudged at her heart. Trying to swallow it away, Elsbeth rubbed Clara's back. 'What about him?'

She lifted her pale face. 'He's going to race King Pig.'

'Don't do this,' Sébastien begged for the tenth time since he'd finally comprehended that Amadeo was serious. Hovering behind him stood Amadeo's father, his stricken face ashen.

But Amadeo was beyond caring. Some things were more important than the monarchy. 'I've told you already, I'm familiar with the car and I know the track like the back of my hand.'

'You've not driven this car on it, or *any* racing car!'

'I've used the simulator.'

'It's not the same thing!'

The test car, which an army of mechanics had been busy doing last-minute safety checks on, was ready. Lowering himself into it, his body wrapped in a spare racing suit, he listened carefully to the chief mechanic's instructions then rammed the helmet on his head.

He switched the engine on and slowly drove it out of the team's garage to the start line.

The news must have spread that the King of Monte Cleure and the heir to the Ceres throne were to race, for the crowd that would usually have dispersed by this point were still in their seats. The television crews had kept their spots too. Let them broadcast it. The more people who witnessed Dominic's humiliation, the better.

Moments later, Dominic appeared from a neighbouring garage in a car with yellow livery, his huge bulk squeezed into a race suit of similar colour.

The red light went on.

Amadeo turned his face to his rival. Even with his helmet on, he could feel Dominic's enmity.

He smiled grimly. King Pig's malevolence had nothing on the revulsion and contempt Amadeo felt for him, an excuse of a man at the forefront of a culture of cruelty, violence and misogyny that had made his wife's life a misery from birth.

Elsbeth's left hand was crushed in Clara's, her right in her mother-in-law's. The eyes of all three were glued to the Queen's television screen before them and the two racing cars, one white, one yellow, waiting side by side for the light to turn green. Marcelo paced the room on his phone, trying to calm Alessia, who was in Madrid with Gabriel.

The light turned green.

Amadeo streaked away, leaving Dominic for dust. Elsbeth knew next to nothing about motor racing but even she could see he was a natural at it, seeming to know when to take it easy and when to put his foot down, reaching speeds so fast her heart accelerated in fright.

She breathed a little easier and imagined the thrills he must be experiencing in this moment, his lifelong dream finally being realised.

What had made him abandon all the rules and protocol about his safety and behaviour to race like this?

'He's bloody amazing,' Marcelo observed in awe as Amadeo finished the first lap fifteen seconds ahead.

All three women nodded without taking their gazes from the screen.

Halfway through the second lap though, and his lead started to slip. The radio communication between Amadeo and the team crackled into life and Amadeo's smooth, irritated voice was broadcast to the world. 'There's something wrong with the accelerator. It's not responding to me.'

Another voice came through but the only words Elsbeth made out were '…pit lane'. The blood was pumping too loudly in her head to hear anything else.

Dominic was fast catching him.

Amadeo moved to the right-hand side of the

track as they approached the final bend before the pit lane. Dominic was now right on his tail.

It happened without warning. Right at the bend, Dominic accelerated past him…but he didn't pass. He swerved and rammed into the side of him.

The noise was ear-piercing.

A cloud of smoke filled the screen, through which a car could be seen flipping in the air and landing vertically, front down, before flopping forwards like a domino.

Elsbeth stared in frozen horror, the shrill yet roaring noise deafening her.

It was only when she felt a tap on her cheek and blinked to find Clara kneeling before her with tears streaming down her face that she realised the deafening sound was her own screams.

There was a banging in Amadeo's head, as if a dozen hammers were smashing into his brain. There was a metallic taste in his mouth too. What the hell had he been drinking? *When* had he been drinking? And why could he smell fire? And where was that whooshing noise coming from?

He tried to lift his head but couldn't move his neck. His legs wouldn't move either.

'Don't move.' The calm voice sounded distant.

He fought to open his eyes. Fought harder. Opened them.

There was pressure on his hand. The voice sounded again. 'Keep still and we'll have you out of here soon. You're going to be fine. Just don't move.'

He tried to focus on the face that the voice and hand belonged to but his vision was blurred. A growing awareness was stealing over him. Not alcohol. An accident.

He couldn't feel his legs.

Fear almost throttled him.

He licked his dry lips and fought for speech. The only word that came was a croaked, 'Elsbeth.'

The world went black.

Amadeo opened his eyes to dazzling bright light.

He must be dead.

He closed his eyes and gave a mental sigh. Strangely, the knowledge he was dead came peacefully to him. Probably because he'd been trained on earth to accept things for the way they were rather than the way he wanted them to be. He hoped the brightness meant that he'd gone up rather than down.

A door opened. He must be in a waiting room.

Soft voices spoke. One of them sounded like Elsbeth.

A fresh wave of peace flooded him. Definitely in a waiting room for heaven. He hoped the angel who sounded like Elsbeth looked like her too. It would be wonderful to see her face one more time. Wonderful to think the angel might move onto the next stage with him as his guide.

There was more peace to know his family would look after her and their baby, but with it sadness to know he would have to wait a long time to meet his child. But maybe up here time moved in a different way than on earth.

The Elsbeth voice spoke again. He slowly turned his face in the direction it came from and opened his eyes again. Joy filled him from his toes to his scalp. The angel sitting beside him looked just like her. Funny though, he'd never thought angels would have blotchy faces from crying.

He cleared his throat. 'How…?'

Angel Elsbeth leaned forwards and placed a gentle finger to his lips. 'Three days. Shh. Try not to speak. The tube hasn't long been taken out of your throat. You'll be sore.'

Now that she mentioned it, his throat *did* hurt.

It was remarkable how alike angel Elsbeth was to real Elsbeth. Identical. Even the shade of blue and expression in her eyes. A tear rolled down the identical cheek and snaked over the identical plump lips. Those same plump lips formed a tremulous smile. 'I thought I'd lost you.' Her hand was laid on his and squeezed. 'But you're going to be okay. You've a broken leg and a shattered hip, three broken ribs, internal injuries and a bruised brain but the doctors are now confident you're going to make a full recovery.'

Forbidden from speaking, incapable of moving,

Amadeo could only gaze intently at the woman he was no longer certain was an angel. Well, not an angel from heaven. If this was the real Elsbeth then she was his angel on earth, and if she was an earth angel then did that mean he wasn't dead after all?

'Dominic's dead.'

He blinked. In his joy of Elsbeth's presence and the pressure of her hand on his, he'd forgotten all about his nemesis.

'They say he died instantly. They put screens around you while they worked to save you.' More tears spilled. 'We didn't know if you were dead or alive for a long time.' She bent over in her chair to lean closer to his face and whisper, 'If you ever do that to me again, I'll kill you myself.'

He turned his hand over in hers and returned the loving pressure.

'I'm not going to let you push me away any more. If you're fearless enough to hurl yourself around a racetrack at over two hundred miles an hour then I can find the courage to fight for us.' The soft, dreamy smile he loved so much curved her cheeks. 'They said that in a moment of consciousness you called my name. You do love me, Amadeo. You love me and I love you, and when we get you out of this place we're going to live together and raise our family together, and every time you try to push me away I will push back, because we belong together and to live without you is to live with a gaping hole in my heart.'

'I'm sorry,' he rasped through his burning throat, using all his strength to squeeze her hand, willing her to believe him.

Her eyes, as soft as her smile, told him she did believe him. Believed him and understood him.

He closed his eyes as the bride who'd walked the aisle towards him all that time ago came into his vision. His heart swelled. Closer she inched, radiating a glow of bliss like the earthly angel she was.

He took his bride's hand and gazed deep into her shining baby blue eyes…

When he next opened his eyes, Elsbeth was curled in her chair asleep, as close to his bed as she could be.

It took three attempts to clear his throat enough to call her name. 'Elsbeth.'

Her eyes snapped open. Met his.

He opened his hand for her. She leaned forward and took it, threading her fingers into his.

He found the strength to raise his other hand and stroke her cheek. 'I love you.' And then his hand dropped and he fell back asleep.

The last of the wounded gap around Elsbeth's heart closed seamlessly, and as she watched the man she loved sleep a dizzying wave of happiness crashed and tumbled through her.

It was a happiness that was to be hers—theirs—for the rest of their lives.

EPILOGUE

AMADEO PUSHED HIS wife's dressing room door open. The hairdresser had plaited Elsbeth's hair and wound it into a coil at the base of her neck and was sliding diamond grips into it.

'Nearly done?' he asked, smiling indulgently at Elsbeth through her reflection at the dressing table mirror. She was still in her silk robe.

'Nearly,' she agreed with an answering smile.

He leaned against the door and watched. To his eyes, his wife needed no beauty tricks but tonight was a state banquet for Elsbeth's cousin, Queen Catalina of Monte Cleure, so all the Berruti women had had their beauty teams dispatched to them.

He still found it strange to remember how this dressing room had once been one of his guest rooms. When he'd been released from hospital and faced months of recovery before he could start undertaking engagements again, he and Elsbeth had sat together with an architect. Within months, their separate quarters had been transformed into

a sprawling home with enough bedrooms to fill
with half a dozen children. He'd given Elsbeth free
rein on the design side. Often he walked through
their sunny yellow day room with its bold furniture and quirky artwork and shook his head at the
sheer pleasure the sight gave him.

The hairdresser slid another grip into the coil
and stepped back. 'That was the last one. Shall I
get Jenna for you?'

'I can help the princess into her dress,' Amadeo
cut in smoothly. 'Tell Jenna she isn't needed.'

'Yes, sir.'

He waited until they were quite alone before
putting his hands on his wife's shoulders.

She arched a brow. 'You're going to help me
dress?'

'I'm going to help you undress first,' he murmured, then dropped a kiss into her neck. 'You
look beautiful.'

She shivered as she always did when he kissed
her there.

He dragged his hands down her arms and slid
them over the swelling of her belly and down to
her pubis. 'Good enough to eat.'

Her mirrored eyes glowed. 'We haven't got
time.' But she did nothing to stop his hands pulling her robe apart and cupping her swollen breasts.

Five years of marriage and still the fever hadn't
broken.

He twisted the swivel chair around so she faced him and dropped to his knees.

Dio, she was ravishing. How he loved to see her pregnant. Loved her. Worshipped the ground she walked on.

He took a breast into his mouth.

She moaned softly and clasped the back of his head. 'We'll be late.'

'So we'll be late. The world will still turn.'

'The children?' she whispered.

His attention went to the other breast. 'Gio's still sleeping, Bella's reading stories with the nanny.'

Then he dragged his mouth down lower and she stopped asking questions.

The stateroom was pulsing with life and music. Elsbeth, heavily pregnant and needing a short breather, had managed to find a place to sit unobserved so she could people-watch. She loved state banquets, especially when a party broke out from them, and tonight's was extra special. It filled her with joy to see so many of the people she loved together, and she gazed at her mother talking animatedly with her stepfather with a happy heart. As soon as her cousin Catalina had taken the Monte Cleure throne, she'd repealed all the cruel and misogynistic laws pertaining to the royal family. Days later, Elsbeth's mother, along with two aunts and three female cousins, had applied for divorce.

Rubbing her belly, she scanned the room for her husband and found him deep in conversation with his brother and brother-in-law. Alessia and Clara were on the dance floor with Bella, Elsbeth's four-year-old treasure, and their children of the same age, Alessia's son Diego and Clara's daughter Sophie, plus Clara's middle daughter, three-year-old Anna. The four children, along with everyone watching, were squealing with laughter as the two princesses taught them the funky chicken dance. From the corner of her eye, Elsbeth spotted her father-in-law mimicking their movements too, and giggled.

Amadeo broke away from the other two men and headed over to her, only the slight limp in his gait evidence of the accident that had almost cost him his life.

Her heart swelled, as it always did when he locked eyes with her. How she loved this man, the father of her children, her lover, her best friend.

'You look happy,' he murmured, sliding into the chair next to her and taking hold of her hand.

Leaning into him, she sighed contentedly. 'Happier than I ever dreamed I could be.'

* * * * *